ROGUE COP

Rogue Cop

WILLIAM P. McGIVERN

Dodd, Mead & Company

NEW YORK

Published by Dodd, Mead & Company, Inc.
79 Madison Avenue, New York, N.Y. 10016

Distributed in Canada by
McClelland and Stewart Limited, Toronto

Manufactured in the United States of America

First Red Badge printing

Library of Congress Catalog Card Number: 54-5986
ISBN: 0-396-08236-X

TO MY MOTHER

ROGUE COP

1

THEY HAD been playing poker for several hours now, not with any particular enthusiasm but simply to kill this quiet stretch of Saturday evening. Later, as the night wore on, the city's tempo would rise to a harder, sharper beat; then murders, knifings and shootings would bring the game to an end. But now the police speaker was silent and the detectives played cards on a cigarette-scarred table in a smoky, unventilated office. Outside, in the large, brightly lighted file room, a clerk was typing up reports, working with severe concentration, stopping only to sip cold black coffee from a cardboard container at his elbow. The glazed-glass door that led to Lieutenant Wilson's office was dark; the lieutenant was out in the districts now, but would be back at Headquarters by ten or eleven. There would be work then for him and his men.

Standing at the brown wooden counter that ran the length of the room was a reporter named Murphy, a bulky, untidily dressed man with a round florid face and thoughtful gray eyes. He was applying himself to the evening paper's crossword puzzle, frowning intently, apparently immune to everything but this immediate preoccupation.

At the card table Sergeant Mike Carmody was dealing now, his big clean hands spraying the cards about with expert speed. He was an arrestingly handsome man in his middle thirties, with a silvering of gray in his thick blond hair. Everything about him looked hard and expensive; his gray flannel suit had cost two hundred dollars and was superbly fitted to his tall, wide-shouldered frame; the planes of his lean tanned face were flat and sharply defined, and his eyes were the cold gray color of winter seas. Even when he smiled there was no softness in it; his smile was a small, direct challenge, a projection of his sure confidence in his own strength and brains.

"Okay, make up your mind," he said to the man on his right. "The spots won't change, Myers."

Myers, a small man with thinning brown hair and a cautious mouth, studied his cards and shook his head slowly. "It's by me, Mike," he said.

The other two players—Abrams, a solemn grandfather and Dirksen, a bean-pole with a thin freckled face—both passed.

Carmody held two queens. He flipped in a half-a-dollar and said, "It's off then." He was bored with the game and made no attempt to conceal it.

Myers and Abrams called the half-dollar bet, but Dirksen threw his cards in. "I haven't seen anything higher than a ten for the last hour," he said, yawning. Then he glanced at Mike Carmody and said conversationally, "Say, Mike, that was a nice pinch your kid brother made the other day. How about that, eh?"

There was a sudden small silence around the table. Carmody studied his cards, ignoring it. "He didn't make the pinch," he said, glancing at Abrams. "How many, Abe?"

"Sure, but he made the identification," Dirksen said. "He caught Delaney with the gun in his hand, but Delaney got away." Dirksen's voice was patient and explicit, as if this were a difficult matter to explain. "Then Delaney got picked up later and your brother made the identification. That's what I meant by saying—"

"I read the story in the paper," Carmody said, catching Dirksen directly with his hard cold eyes. He smiled then, the bright quick smile in which there was no warmth or humor. "But we're playing cards now, remember?"

"Well, I'm not stopping you," Dirksen said, shrugging and looking away from Carmody's eyes.

"That's fine," Carmody said, still smiling. He wondered fleetingly if Dirksen had been needling him; Dirksen was dumb enough to try it, after all.

Myers took one card, Abrams three. Carmody drew three to his pair of queens and without looking at them pushed in a dollar. He wasn't interested in Myers' one-card draw. If Myers caught a flush or straight he'd raise, but the amount involved wasn't enough to buy a decent steak. Myers caught. Carmody guessed that from the way his eyes flicked from his cards to his little heap of money.

"I'll bump it five," Myers said.

"You can't," Abrams said. "The limit is two."

"Who said anything about a limit?" Myers demanded.

"Well, it's always been a limit," Abrams said, shrugging his big shoulders. "But it don't make any difference to me. I'm out."

"We didn't establish a limit tonight," Myers said, wetting his lips and glancing at Carmody.

"Make it five if you want," Carmody said, only slightly irritated. Myers had hooked and now he wanted to get rich on one hand. Let him, he thought. Glancing at his cards he found that he had drawn another queen to go with his openers, and a pair of tens. He grinned at the fantastic luck and tossed in ten dollars. "Once again, my friend," he said.

"You're bluffing," Myers said. He stared into Carmody's hard quick smile, trying to keep a weary premonition of defeat from showing in his face.

"Raise then," Carmody said.

"I'll just call," Myers said, pushing in his last five dollars. He had to use silver to make up the amount, and then he put down a king-high straight and looked hopefully at Carmody.

Carmody stared at his cinch hand. He knew all about Myers, as he knew about all the detectives on his shift. The damn fool had two young daughters, and a wife in a sanitarium, but here he was throwing away fifteen dollars in one hand of poker.

Carmody hesitated, annoyed with himself, and Myers watched him with mounting confidence.

"Come on," Myers said. "What've you got?"

"It's your money," Carmody said shortly, and tossed his cards in, face down. The gesture would be wasted, he thought, as he leaned back and lit a cigarette. Myers, pulling in his money triumphantly now, was like most cops, brave, honest and dumb. Carmody felt no sympathy for him, only a blend of exasperation and anger.

He'd never have a cent more than his salary and not even that unless he learned to stop drawing to inside straights. That's what bothered him, Carmody thought, his face expressionless. Myers was a fool and he didn't like fools.

"Caught you bluffing, didn't I?" Myers said, arranging his money happily. "Thought you could run me out with a five-dollar bet, eh? Well, my luck's changing. I'm starting back now, remember that."

"You'd better start by remembering the limit," Carmody said, his irritation sharpened by Myers' yapping. "You won't get rich by changing the rules in the middle of a deal."

"Is that how you got rich?" Myers said, stung by Carmody's tone. "By following the rules?"

There was tense silence then, as if everyone at the table had suddenly held his breath. Myers had skated onto thin ice; he was on an area that had mile-high danger signs posted on it. The unnatural silence lasted until Carmody said very quietly, "Let's play cards, Myers. It's your deal, I think."

"Sure, that's right," Myers said, and began quickly to shuffle the cards. There was a white line showing around his small cautious mouth.

Murphy, the reporter, drifted and leaned against the doorway, hat pushed back on his head, a little smile on his big florid face. "I should have been a cop," he said sighing. "Nothing to worry about but filling straights."

No one answered him.

"Say, when's Delaney's trial?" he asked of no one in particular.

Dirksen looked up at him, his freckled face blank and innocent. "Next month sometime, I guess. That right, Mike?"

Carmody nodded slowly, studying his cards. "That's right. The thirteenth."

"The unlucky thirteenth for Delaney," Murphy said, watching Carmody's sharp handsome profile. "That should be a big day for your brother, Mike. Any cop would be happy to finger a hoodlum like Delaney."

"I'd be glad of the chance," Myers said, risking a quick glance at Carmody.

They were needling him cautiously, a dangerous pastime, cautiously or any other way. He knew they were watching him over their cards, ready to drop their eyes swiftly if he raised his head.

Without looking up he said quietly, "Murph, we just got through talking about my brother's case. We kind of exhausted the subject, too. So why don't you run off and find a good exciting accident to cover? Let us play our little game in peace."

Murphy smiled and raised his hat to Carmody. "I depart, O Sergeant," he said, his thoughtful eyes contradicting the smile on his lips. "The city calls me. Full of heartbreak and tragedy, but laced with dark laughter withall, it beckons and whispers that its secrets are mine."

Carmody smiled slightly. "Why don't you try that to music?"

"Good idea. Music is getting popular in town," Murphy said in a changed voice. "Singing particularly. Maybe even Delaney will take it up. Well, adios, chums."

He strolled out and Dirksen shook his head. "Odd ball," he murmured.

Carmody swallowed a dryness in his throat and said, "Okay, let's play cards."

Ten minutes later the phone in the file room rang. The clerk answered it, listened for a few seconds, then said, "Yes, sir. Right away." Covering the receiver with the palm of his hand, he called out, "Sarge, a call for you."

"Who is it?" Carmody said.

"Dan Beaumonte."

There was another little silence at the card table. Carmody stared at his cards for a few seconds, then tossed them in. "Deal me out," he said, and walked into the file room, moving with an easy controlled grace that was somehow menacing in a man of his size.

Abrams began to whistle softly through his teeth. The three detectives avoided one another's eyes, but their ears were turned to the open door of the file room.

Carmody lifted the phone and said, "Hello, Dan. How're things?"

"It was a bad day," Beaumonte said. His voice was deep and rich, stirred gently by an undercurrent of humor. "I had three tips at Jamaica but they all ran out. Do you know of any glue factory that's looking for three good specimens?"

"It's a good thing to get a day like that behind you," Carmody said. He knew what Beaumonte wanted and he wished he'd get to it; but you didn't hurry Beaumonte.

Then it came. "I want to see you tonight, Mike. You're working four-to-twelve?"

"That's right."

"Twelve is too late. How about making it now? I'm at my apartment."

Carmody knew the clerk and the detectives at the card table were listening. "Well, I'll see you around," he said.

"Right away, Mike. He's your brother."

"Sure."

He put the phone down and walked back to the smoke-filled card room. Dirksen began talking loudly. "The thing is, you can't figure the odds in Hi-Lo poker. You never know, for instance, whether—"

"I'm going out," Carmody said to Abrams. "Take over till I get back."

"Okay, Sarge."

"Tell the lieutenant when he comes in that I'll be about an hour."

Dirksen smiled as Carmody buttoned his shirt collar and pulled up his tie. "I wish I got calls from big men like Beaumonte," he said. "That'd make me feel like a real operator."

Carmody guessed that Dirksen was trying to be funny but he was in no mood for it. He put his big fists on the table and leaned forward, fixing Dirksen with his hard, bright smile. "Now listen to me," he said gently. "If you want to talk about telephone calls talk about your own. Get your wife to call you and talk about that. But stop talking about mine. Okay?"

Dirksen's freckled face got red. "Hell, there's nothing to be touchy about," he said. "I just passed a remark. It's still a free country, ain't it?"

Carmody smiled and let the tension dissolve. "Free

country? Try that on your landlord and grocer and see what happens."

A relieved laugh went around the table. Carmody straightened up and said, "Take it easy, I'll see you later."

He went downstairs, walked past the House Sergeant's office and through the silent roll call room, where the Magistrate's bench loomed up like an alter in the darkness.

Outside on the sidewalk he paused, savoring the welcome freshness of the spring air against his face. From here, at the north entrance of City Hall, he looked down the glittering length of Market Street, blazing with light against the black sky. The Saturday night crowd jammed the sidewalks, and the traffic was flowing in thick, noisy streams. Somewhere off to his right a police siren was screaming faintly. West, he thought, the Tenth district. He nodded to three patrolmen who went by him on the way to work, and then lit a cigarette and walked down the block to his long gray convertible.

The traffic made his trip across town slow and difficult; but he was grateful for the time it gave him to think. He had done a lot of thinking in the past week, but now he was meeting Beaumonte and the chips would be down. Thinking wouldn't be enough; there had to be a solution. He stared through the windshield, turning the problem around slowly in his clear, alert mind. Waiting at a stop light, he suddenly pounded his big fist on the rim of the steering wheel. If only his brother hadn't identified Delaney. Anyone but Eddie. And if only

Delaney weren't threatening to sing. If only a hundred things.

The trouble stemmed from the fact that Delaney worked for a gambler and racketeer named Dan Beaumonte.

And so did Mike Carmody.

There was a girl standing at the terrace window when Carmody walked into Beaumonte's long, elegantly appointed living room. She turned slowly, smiling at him, her figure slim and graceful against the backdrop of the lighted city.

"Hello, Mike. Come over and look at our little village. It's like being high up in a castle."

Carmody joined her and they inspected the view for a few seconds in silence. The city was beautiful now, the lights spreading over it like an immense sparkling carpet. Beaumonte's apartment was on the twenty-fifth floor of a massive building which overlooked the park and a long curving stretch of the river. Like a castle, Carmody thought. With a safe view of the slaves.

"Where's Beaumonte?" he asked her.

"Changing. Would you like a drink?"

"No, thanks."

She patted his arm and he saw that she was a little tight. "I hate to drink alone. Dan says that's my trouble. But what's a girl to do when she's alone?"

"Have a drink, I guess," Carmody said.

"Absolutely right," she said, and poked him in the chest with her finger. "You don't mind if I go ahead?"

"Not a bit." Carmody felt vaguely irritated as he watched her stroll to the bar. Not with her or Beaumonte, but with himself for some curious reason. The girl's name was Nancy Drake, and she had been Beaumonte's mistress for years. She was a slender blonde with piquant, good-natured features and fine gray eyes. Everything about her blended neatly with the perfection of the room; the oil paintings, the balanced groups of furniture, the nice integration of form and color, were all an appropriate backdrop for her pale, well-cared-for beauty. It made a pretty picture, Carmody thought. Well-organized luxury without time payments or mortgages. The room and the girl had been bought and paid for by Beaumonte with good hard cash.

This was what irritated him, Carmody decided. The room looked like an art gallery and Nancy looked like the daughter of a duke. It was the big lie that disgusted him; they should do their business in the back of a saloon, and if women were present they should be the kind who hung around saloons. But it was Beaumonte's lie so that made it all right.

Carmody realized his thoughts were running in illogical circles. Why should he object to Beaumonte's pretenses? Weren't his own just as bad? But he was a little sick of Beaumonte at the moment and he didn't bother applying logic to his judgments. When I'm fed up I'll walk out, he told himself, frowning slightly, disturbed by his thoughts. I'm not in so deep that I can't take a walk.

A door opened and Beaumonte came into the room. He held a slim cigar in one hand and wore a dinner jacket cut of black raw silk.

"Sorry to keep you waiting, Mike," he said, in his deep rich voice. "I'm glad you could get right over."

Carmody said something appropriate and watched Beaumonte as he put an arm around Nancy's waist and kissed her bare shoulder. Sometimes Beaumonte's expression gave him away; but there was nothing to learn from it now. He seemed in good spirits but his mood could change drastically and without warning, Carmody knew.

Physically, Beaumonte was impressive, with a big well-padded body, thick gray hair and a complexion like that of a well-cared-for baby. His lips were full and red, his brown eyes clear and untroubled. He spent about a third of each day taking steam baths, sun-lamp treatments and suffering the ministrations of his barber, masseur and trainer. His manner was sensuous and complacent; he could bear nothing but silk against his skin, and fussed pretentiously with his chef on the subjects of sauces and wines. There were times when Carmody half expected him to start stroking himself or purring.

"Mike won't drink," Nancy said.

"Not a bad habit," Beaumonte said, glancing at her appraisingly.

"I'm okay," she said.

"Yeah, so far. Won't change your mind, Mike?"

"All right, make it a mild Scotch," Carmody said.

"I'll have sherry, the Spanish with the crowns on the label," Beaumonte told Nancy. He glanced at Carmody. "It's a fine one. I have it imported especially. You have to watch sherry, Mike. It's splendid when it's right. But when it isn't, I mean if it's off even a shade, well it's not worth drinking."

"Sure," Carmody said, managing to keep his annoyance from showing in his face. Beaumonte had grown up on bootleg whiskey; he had been a small-time hoodlum in the Thirties, a skinny punk in pin-striped suits and a gray fedora, which he wore pulled down all around in the style favored by Capone's bums in Chicago. Money, carloads of it, had brought out the art lover and wine bibber.

Nancy brought their drinks on a round silver tray, and Beaumonte's expression changed as he noticed that she had made herself another highball. "You've had enough," he said. "Leave that here and go lie down."

"Dan, don't be dull," she said, trying to soften his face with an impudent, gamin smile. "You'll spoil the party."

"You've had your ration for today," he said, and now he meant business. His face and manner were unpleasant. "It's sloshing in the scuppers. Beat it. Sleep it off."

"All right, Dan," she said quickly, her little pose melting under the hard anger in his eyes. "So long, Mike."

Here was the art patron and wine sipper, Carmody thought, and the irony of it was enough to check his irritation. For some reason Beaumonte enjoyed humiliating her; and by a freak of timing the scenes always seemed to occur when he was playing the grand gentleman to the hilt. Maybe she planned it that way, Carmody thought. Beaumonte had picked her out of a chorus line six years ago, and since that time had transformed her into a lady. She had been trained to walk and talk, to manage a dinner party for thirty and to dress herself with quiet taste. Beaumonte had hired trainers and coaches for her, he had schooled her like an intelligent dog until she could perform any social trick with ease. And somewhere on the way she had started hitting the bottle. She would probably be dead in five years, Carmody knew, and he wondered if that was why Beaumonte was so rough on her. Because the investment wasn't paying off; the bought-and-paid-for little lady had crossed him by turning into a lush. But there was something else, Carmody guessed. Beaumonte would have enjoyed humiliating a real lady, but no genuine article would take it; so he had created Nancy as a stand-in for the real thing. By hurting her he took a small revenge against a class which had always intimidated him; people whose English was correct and whose manners were casual and right.

Beaumonte sat down in a deep chair, the glass of sherry in one hand, the slim cigar in the other. He looked up at Carmody, a small frown gathering on his pampered features. "Let's get right to it, Mike. Sit down and get comfortable." He sipped some of the sherry and wet his full lips. Then he turned his clear brown eyes directly to Carmody. "It's this, Mike. If your brother fingers Delaney it can cause us trouble. Because Delaney has told our lawyer that he's going to talk, unless we take him off the hook. So your brother's got to be sensible. You understand?"

Carmody shrugged his wide shoulders and said nothing. The silence stretched out awkwardly until Beaumonte, still frowning, said, "Well, do you see it?"

"Part of it," Carmody said. "What's the rest of it?"

"All right, let's start at the start," Beaumonte said, settling in the chair and crossing his fat legs. "Delaney, who's worked for us off and on for years, shot and killed a man named Ettonberg. That was last month. It was a stupid murder, and not tied up with us in any way. Ettonberg and Delaney had a fight about a woman and Delaney killed him after he'd been drinking so much that he couldn't hit the ground with his hat. As you know, this happened in a boardinghouse on your brother's beat. He went in and found Delaney standing over Ettonberg with a gun in his hand. If he'd killed the bastard right then, he'd have done us a favor. But Delaney slugged your brother and got away without being seen by anyone else. So he went to Martin's joint where there was a poker game and fixed himself up an alibi."

"I guess we both know the story pretty well," Carmody said. "The cops picked up Delaney on my brother's description. Eddie testified at the Grand Jury hearing and the D.A. got a true bill."

"Okay, now we're up to the present," Beaumonte said. "When Delaney goes to trial your brother can finger him right into the chair. And that can't happen. If it does, Delaney talks."

What did Delaney know? Carmody wondered. "Can he hurt you by talking?" he asked.

Beaumonte looked annoyed. "Don't talk about me being hurt. I don't like that kind of talk."

Carmody shrugged. "No point in not being realistic. I talk pretty damn much."

"We're going to save Delaney," Beaumonte said. Carmody's remark had brought spots of color into his cheeks, but he didn't let his anger get him away from the subject. "So you talk to your brother, Mike?"

"What do I tell him?"

"You tell him he don't identify Delaney at the trial."

"Will that do any good?" Carmody said. "My brother has already testified against Delaney at the Grand Jury hearing."

"Don't you worry about the legal end of it," Beaumonte said. "That's what we pay lawyers for. And here's the way they've figured it. Delaney's attorney waived a hearing before the Magistrate the night of the murder. So your brother didn't have to identify him then. Naturally, Delaney was held for the Grand Jury without bail. In this state defendants don't appear at the Grand Jury hearings, so your brother didn't confront Delaney and make an identification. He just testified that to the best of his knowledge a man named Delaney was standing over Ettonberg's dead body when he came on the scene. That gave the D.A. his true bill. Your brother won't confront Delaney until the trial. And that's when he blows the case up by refusing to finger him."

"It will look raw as hell," Carmody said.

"To hell with how it looks," Beaumonte said angrily. "They'll know he's lying but they won't be able to prove it. The jury is what counts. And our attorneys will make them believe that your brother's an honest cop who won't send an innocent man to the chair just to fatten up some D.A.'s score of convictions. Delaney will beat the rap. And, by God, Mike, he's got to beat this rap. You understand?"

"They'll boot my brother off the force."

"So is that bad? We'll take care of him. Offer him ten thousand to start with, and see what he thinks of it. And we can go higher. A lot higher."

Carmody hesitated a moment. Then he said, "Why do you want me to handle it, Dan?" A phrase came into his mind from his forgotten religion and forgotten values: "*Let this chalice pass from me!*" He didn't want this job, and in some intuitive manner he was afraid of it. But there was no one he could ask for help. Not Beaumonte, that was certain. And there was no one else. *Let this chalice . . .* Why had those words occurred to him?

Beaumonte was rolling the cigar between his full red lips, watching him carefully. "I want you to handle it because it's a big job," he said at last. "I'll tell you this: Ackerman is watching it personally."

Carmody nodded slowly. It was important then, no doubt of it. Ackerman was number one. He controlled the city's gambling and numbers racket. Beaumonte ran the west side personally, and acted as a link between Ackerman and the other districts; he supervised the operations of Fanzo in Central, Nick Boyle in Meadowstrip, and Lockwood in the Northeast. But all of it was under Ackerman's thumb. He juggled the judges and magistrates and cops, he put the collar on the politicians he needed and he fought the reform movement on the high inside levels. Thinking about it, Carmody felt a brush of anxiety; there was a lot of muscle stacked up against his brother.

"Why is Ackerman so interested?" Carmody asked.

Beaumonte was silent a moment. Then he said quietly, "Don't start guessing about him. You know that's stupid.

Just remember he's interested. That's enough. Now there's one other point. I don't want any hard feelings between you and me."

"I don't get that," Carmody said.

Beaumonte got to his feet and glanced at his gold wrist watch. "Hell, it's later than I thought," he said. Carmody had risen also and Beaumonte put a hand on his arm, turning him toward the door. "This thing has got to be handled, one way or the other," he said. "I want it peaceful. I hope your brother is smart and winds up with a nice little bundle in his pocket." They stopped at the door, facing each other, and something had changed in Beaumonte's smooth plump face. He was still smiling but the smile meant nothing now. "We're not kids, Mike," he said. "I'm putting it on the line. If your brother don't play ball we'll have to handle it our way. That's why you're making the first pitch. If you don't sell him the deal, you can't blame us for doing what we got to do. Is that clear enough?"

"I'll talk to my brother," Carmody said evenly.

"How do you get along with him?"

"So-so."

"What's the matter? He's your kid brother, he should do what you tell him."

"We don't see much of each other," Carmody said.

"That's too bad." Beaumonte looked at him, his head tilted slightly. "Don't he like your friends?"

"Lots of people don't," Carmody said, holding his irritation in check.

"Not smart people," Beaumonte said, smiling. "When'll you see him?"

"As soon as I can."

"Make it tonight. He doesn't go to work until twelve."

"How do you know?"

Beaumonte shrugged. "I told you this was important. We're keeping tabs on him. You see him now, then come back. I'll be here all night. Got that?"

Carmody hesitated. "Okay, Dan," he said finally.

Beaumonte smiled. "We want this peaceful. **Good luck.**"

2

CARMODY DROVE from Beaumonte's apartment to a drug store on Market Street and called his brother's home. There was no answer. He replaced the receiver and remained seated in the booth, thinking coolly and without emotion of Beaumonte's words: *We want this peaceful . . . but if your brother won't play ball we'll have to do it our way.*

Beaumonte meant that. There was no phoniness about him when it came to business. He squandered his bluff on paintings and horse shows and the Mayor's council on human relations, catering generously then to his itch for approval and respectability. But this was business. His and Ackerman's. And they'd order Eddie killed with no more emotion than they'd order a steak.

Carmody wasn't worried yet. The confidence in his own strength and brains was the hard core of his being, impervious to strain or pressure. Somehow, he would save Eddie. He accepted Beaumonte's deadly injunction as a factor in the equation. They—Beaumonte and Ackerman—meant business. Therefore, something else would have to give. That was Eddie.

After a ten-minute wait he dialed Eddie's number again and let it ring. Eddie might be outside watering the lawn, or at the workbench in the basement, repairing a lock or mending a screen. Something important, Carmody thought.

The phone clicked in his ear. Eddie's voice said, "Yes? Hello."

"This is Mike. How's the boy?"

"Mike? How are you?" Eddie's tone was neutral, neither friendly nor unfriendly. "I was splicing a hose out in the back yard. You been ringing long?"

Splicing a hose, Carmody thought, shaking his head. "Eddie, I want to see you tonight."

"I'm going out pretty soon," his brother said.

"Well, I can meet you anywhere you say. This is important. Where will you be?"

"Vespers at Saint Pat's."

"Vespers?"

"Sure. You might remember if you put your mind to it."

Eddie's tone, hard and sarcastic, warned Carmody off the subject. "How about afterward then?" he said.

There was a short silence. Then Eddie said, "I've got a date later, Mike."

"Well, something you've been keeping from me, eh?" Carmody said, trying for a lighter touch.

"I know what's on your mind," Eddie said shortly. "And the answer is no, Mike."

"Don't jump to conclusions," Carmody said. This was no time for anger; that would tear it for good. "I've got something to tell you in person. So how about it?"

"Okay," Eddie said, after a pause. "There's a club at Edgely and Broad called the Fanfair. I can meet you there at one."

"Fine." He tried once more for a lighter mood. "You're moving in swanky circles, kid."

"It's just a neighborhood joint," Eddie said, keeping it cold and distant. "I'll see you, Mike."

Carmody left the booth and glanced at his watch. It was almost eight-thirty and there was no point in going back to Headquarters. He ordered a lemon Coke at the fountain and looked over the magazine rack while he drank it. Then he phoned in and left a message with the clerk for Lieutenant Wilson, saying he was on something important and would be in later. The clerk told him everything was still quiet, and added that the card game could go on all night if things stayed this way.

"Yes, we've got snap jobs," Carmody said, and replaced the receiver.

With almost two hours to kill, he left the drug store and strolled down Market, trying to dismiss the memory of Eddie's coldness. It hadn't always been that way. Carmody was eight years older than his brother and as a boy Eddie had idolized him, which was inevitable, considering the difference in their ages. He had taught Eddie to swim, to play ball, to fight and had bought him clothes and lent him money for his first dates. Eddie had been a nice little guy, Carmody thought, walking along the bright crowded street. A serious kid, not bright or shrewd but straightforward and dependable. Almost too pretty in the soft, dark-pale Irish manner; flawless fair skin, long-lashed blue eyes, thick, curly black hair. In his cassock and surplice with the round white collar under his chin he had always stolen the show at St. Pat's Christmas and Easter processions. But he'd never been spoiled, Carmody remembered. He was just a likable little boy, shyly earnest and direct, with a thousand little-boy questions always buzzing in his head. Carmody smiled slightly. *Why don't footballs float like balloons? Could the old man lick Jack Dempsey? How come you have to leave home when you marry an old girl?* Carmody had always felt like smiling at him when he asked questions like that, his face serious, his long-lashed eyes staring at Mike as if he knew everything in the world. They'd got along fine then and maybe that was the only way two people ever got along—when one of them was so trusting that he accepted the other's every word without doubt or resentment. But it couldn't stay that way. Eventually, the dumb one got smart and saw that his idol was just another poor fool.

Time was standing still, Carmody thought, looking at his watch. The crowds went by him, charged with night time excitement and a traffic cop waved and gave him a soft, smiling salute. He crossed the street and stopped to look at the bright posters in front of a movie house. Buying a ticket, he went inside and took a back seat. The audience sloped down from him to the screen, a dark, intense unit. There was an irritating smell of stale smoke and popcorn in the heavy air.

After twenty minutes he lost interest in the picture and left. It was the kind of junk that annoyed him thoroughly, a sticky, phony story about a man and woman who ran into trouble because they ignored the standards of their society. Who in hell made those standards? A group of frightened ninnies who clung for protection to the symbols of reversed collars and nightsticks, and wanted only a kind boss, an insurance policy and a two-room apartment with babies.

There was no penalty for smashing the rules made by these timid people; Carmody had proved that to his satisfaction. The truth they gave lip-service to didn't exist; there was no mystery about life, no hidden value, no far-away beauty and happiness. The true life spread around every human being, a dog-eat-dog slaughter for money and power. Those who didn't see it were blinded by fear; they closed their eyes to the truth because they were afraid to fight. They wanted a handout, a pension, a break, from some other world. They can't take this world, and that's why we take it away from them, Carmody thought.

Finally, he turned into a night club on Fifteenth Street, a big splashy place with a name band and a Hollywood star doing an M.C. turn between pictures. Carmody had a drink with the owner, a worried little man named Ventura, who was going into court the following month to explain some tax irregularities. They talked about the case and Ventura wanted to know if Carmody had heard anything about it, or did he know the judge, and how the hell did things look anyway?

"That's all Federal," Carmody said, relieved that there was no way he could help. That was odd; normally he didn't mind doing a favor. Maybe I want a favor, he thought. But what? And who can help me? While Ventura was off greeting a chattering bunch of expensive-looking college kids, Carmody paid the check and left.

Now it was time to see his brother.

Eddie was sitting at the bar, his broad back entrance, and Carmody came up behind h. slapped him on the shoulder. His brother turned, smiling awkwardly, and they exchanged hellos and shook hands.

"What'll you have?" Eddie asked him.

"It doesn't matter. Scotch, I guess."

"I'll coast on this," Eddie said, nodding at his half-filled glass of beer.

The Fanfair was a pleasant spot, several notches above a neighborhood tavern. There was a piano on a dais at the end of the long bar and beyond that double doors led to the dining room. The lighting was soft and the decorations were attractive; it was the sort of place a young man would take his girl after the movies, or where a married couple would bring their in-laws for Sunday dinner. There was no bouncer, no drunks or cigarette girls, no unescorted women.

"Let's take a booth," Carmody suggested.

"Sure." Eddie picked up his beer and crossed to a row of dark-wood booths, moving with solid strides that were in sharp contrast to Carmody's easy but powerful grace. Eddie was several inches shorter than his brother, but his shoulders were heavier. At twenty-eight he was in good shape, but he would have trouble with his weight in a few years. There was still the suggestion of the choir boy in his square pale face and in the shyly earnest expression around his eyes. Despite his bulk, there was a vulnerable look about him; he had never learned to camouflage his emotions. His hopes and hurts and disappointments were nakedly apparent, mirrored for everyone to see in his embarrassingly clear and honest eyes.

"What's on your mind, Mike?" Eddie said, after a quick glance over his shoulder at the piano.

"Does your girl work here?"

"Yes, she's a singer and plays her own accompaniments." Eddie smiled. "She's pretty good, I guess."

He was very proud of her, Carmody saw. "Well, let's get this over with," he said, moving his glass aside, fixing Eddie with his hard eyes. "You got yourself into a mess on this Delaney business."

"That's your version of it, not mine."

"Damn it, let me finish," Carmody said. "Delaney's in a position to embarrass the men who run the city. He's threatening to talk unless they take the heat off. You're the heat, Eddie. Do you understand?"

Eddie put his elbows on the table and leaned closer to Carmody. "You want me to say it wasn't Delaney I saw standing over Ettonberg with a gun in his hand? Is that what you want?"

"I want to keep you out of trouble," Carmody said.

"Thanks all to hell," Eddie said shortly. "I don't need your help."

"Kid, be sensible. Why be a hero for a bum like Delaney?"

"If he's such a bum, why are the big boys worried?"

"He can embarrass them; put it that way."

"They embarrass real easy, don't they?" Eddie said.

"Be a humorist," Carmody said dryly. "But see if this strikes you as comical. Unless you testify sensibly, you won't testify at all."

Eddie stared at him for a few seconds, his big chest rising and falling rapidly. "I'll get killed for doing my job," he said at last. "Is that what you're telling me?"

"I'm just a carrier pigeon, a Western Union boy," Carmody said. "I'm delivering a message. But you wouldn't be getting this treatment if it weren't for me. They'd step on you like a bug if you weren't my brother."

"I owe you a lot," Eddie said bitterly. "I get a reprieve because my brother works with the big boys."

"Don't talk like a fool." They were both becoming angry and Carmody knew that would ruin everything. He lit a cigarette and drew a long breath. This always happened with him and Eddie; he could handle other men without his emotions interfering, but this kid brother of his always got under his skin. Eddie was too stubborn to see the truth, and that made Carmody furious. "Now look," he said, keeping his temper in check. "You're not just getting a reprieve. You'll get ten thousand bucks to go with it, which is more dough than you can save in twenty years pulling police boxes. You get that for just saying, 'I'm not sure' when you look at Delaney in court."

"I'll tell the truth so to hell with you," Eddie said, his big hands tightening into fists. He was bitterly angry but beneath that was a deeper feeling; his soft clear eyes were like those of a child who has been hurt by a trusted adult.

A chord sounded from the piano and he turned his head quickly.

The big baby, Carmody thought helplessly. He doesn't understand how the world is run, he doesn't know anything except the nonsense the old man pounded into him. Carmody wondered how he would handle this as he glanced past Eddie to the girl at the piano. She was older than Eddie, thirty or thirty-two maybe, a slender girl with brown hair and a small serious face. She began to sing a sentimental ballad in a voice that was low and pleasant, but not much else. Carmody wondered what her appeal was to Eddie. What would his brother want in a woman? Carmody didn't know. They had stopped communicating on all but superficial levels long before he got to know Eddie's needs and taste in women. This one didn't seem to be the party type. She looked brave and thoughtful, but that might be part of the act. She wasn't voluptuous or sexy, in fact she didn't even look very strong; her arms were white and thin againt her black evening gown, and he could see the deep shadowed hollow at the base of her throat. A demure clinging vine maybe. Would Eddie like that? Someone he could baby and protect? Carmody sipped his drink and shook his head. That would be a great union. Two babies hugging each other in the big windy world.

Something about her touched a faint responsive chord in his memory. There was a teasing familiarity in the way she sat at the piano, her back perfectly straight, thin shoulders squared and her small head raised as if watching for something on the horizon. Carmody ran her face and body through his mind as if it were a fingerprint card in a selector machine. He tried to match her up with friends and enemies, with places and crimes, but the effort produced no answer to the little query in his mind.

"She's good," he said to Eddie, making it warm and friendly. "What's her name?"

"Karen Stephanson."

That meant nothing to Carmody. "Is she a local product?"

"No, she was born in New York. But she's worked all over the country, I guess."

"How did you get to know her?"

"Well, this place used to be on my beat. I came by one night when it was raining and she was waiting for a cab. She lives near here, at the Empire Hotel. I called the district from the pull box and got one of the squads to drive her home."

Carmody smiled. "Very neat!"

"Well, I stopped in to hear her sing a few times, and then asked her for a date. That's all there was to it."

"Is this a serious deal?"

"With me it is. I don't know about her."

Carmody patted his brother's shoulder, still smiling. "Look, if any ninety-eight-pound female thinks she is too good for you just tell her about the Kings of Ireland. Hell man, we're direct descendants."

"Don't forget the family castles and hunting lodges," Eddie said, responding to the lighter mood. "There must be castles every square yard over there. I never met a Mick whose family didn't own one or two at least."

Smiling at him, Carmody thought, he's serious, all right. And with Eddie that wouldn't mean one-night stands. He'd want it all the way, with an apartment, babies, diapers on the radiators, the works. "You want to marry her?" he asked.

"I guess I would," Eddie said, coloring slightly.

"Good, keep that in mind," Carmody said. "Now without getting sore, let's go back to Delaney."

"We've settled that," Eddie said shortly, his mood changing.

"Listen to me, damn you. You won't marry anybody unless you play ball. Get that through your thick head. You'll be dead." I've got to sell him this, Carmody thought, but for the first time he felt a tug of anxiety. Supposing he couldn't? What then?

"Let's drop it," Eddie said angrily. Then his face softened, and his eyes became helpless and vulnerable. "I'm not judging you, Mike. Maybe you're the smart one. And maybe I'm a dope, like you say. But I like it the way I am. Can't you see that? I don't like fighting you. It gives me a charge to see you, and to kid around about the Kings of Ireland. That's fine, for some reason. But let's drop this other thing."

"If I do you get killed."

Eddie smiled crookedly. "Well, I haven't anything too big on my conscience."

"Damn it, stop talking like the old man," Carmody said, snapping out the words. "What about this girl?" Will you do her any good lying on a morgue slab?"

"Leave the old man out of this," Eddie said.

"Okay, forget him. But stop talking like a child."

"I'm no child. I can handle myself."

"Dear God," Carmody said, raising his eyes to the ceiling. "Now you're going to be a hero. Stand right up to a crowd that just about holds the whole state in its hands."

"Maybe I'm not so alone as you think," Eddie said. "Supposing I go to Superintendent Shortall with your deal. What about that?"

Carmody smiled gently. "Shortall's no knight in armor. He works for the same boss as I do."

"That's not straight."

"Wouldn't I be likely to know?"

Eddie stared at him, swallowing hard. Then he said bitterly, "Yeah, you'd know about that, I guess. So Shortall is on the take too." He suddenly pounded a fist on the table. "The big phony. Him and his speeches about our responsibility to the community, about being good citizens first and good cops second."

"Fine, get mad," Carmody said, nodding approvingly. "That's a healthy reaction. It's the first step toward getting smart. Now listen to me," he said, fixing Eddie with his cold hard eyes. "I've been through all this. Do you think they'll let you be a good cop? Sure, if you don't bother them. You can be as efficient as you like on school crossings, but they'll break you in two if you stick your nose into their business."

Watching Eddie's troubled face, Carmody realized that it was time to ease off, to let the seed he had planted grow. "What happened to our drinks?" he said. "Let's have another round; okay?"

"Does that include me?"

It was the girl, Karen, who spoke. She was standing beside their booth, smiling pleasantly at Eddie.

"Good gosh, I didn't even notice you'd stopped singing," Eddie said, and started to get to his feet. But she put a hand lightly on his shoulder and said, "Never mind, I'll slide in beside you."

"This is my brother, Mike, Karen. Mike, this is Karen."

They smiled at each other, and Carmody said, "What would you like to drink?"

"Scotch, please. On the rocks."

Carmody gave the waiter their order, then looked at Karen. "We were just talking about you in connection with Kings of Ireland," he said.

"Cut it out, Mike," Eddie said, grinning uncomfortably.

"I don't understand. Should I?" Karen said, smiling at Eddie.

"No, it was just a gag," he said.

She's a cool little cookie, Carmody thought, studying her with interest.

She realized that he was taking her measure but it didn't disturb her; she sipped her drink slowly and gave him time to draw his conclusions. There were girls who would have resented his deliberate appraisal, but her manner remained poised and friendly. She was better-looking up close, he thought. Her eyes were very lovely, deeply blue and steady, and there was a hint of intelligence and humor in the turn of her soft, gently curving lips. She wore her brown hair parted in the middle and clipped behind with a small silver barette. Against the dark wood of the booth her bare shoulders were white and square. She held herself very handsomely, chin raised, back straight and her hands resting in her lap.

They talked casually until Eddie glanced at his watch.

"I'm taking Karen out for a sandwich, Mike," he said. "This is her only break before she gets through at two."

"Perhaps Mike would like to come with us." She spoke to Eddie but she was watching Carmody, taking his measure as he had taken hers.

"No, I've got to get back downtown," he said, knowing Eddie didn't want him along. Karen understood that, he saw. She finished her drink and put out her cigarette, changing the mood with these little gestures. "We'd better go then, I think," she said.

Carmody paid the check. Karen excused herself to get a wrap and Eddie went off to make a phone call. Carmody stood alone, flipping a coin in one hand, and staring at his tall, wide-shouldered figure in the bar mirror. He'd made a good start. Eddie had something to think about now, and when a man started thinking he was usually getting on the right track.

He turned, still flipping the coin, and saw Karen coming toward him with light quick steps. She carried a stole over one arm and he could hear the click of her high-heeled sandals above the murmur of laughter and conversation. And then he noticed that she was limping. It was a very small limp, just a slight favoring of her left leg, but the sight of it touched the responsive chord in his mind. Where had he seen her before? Then, when she stopped and smiled briefly at him, the cogs in his sharp brain meshed together smoothly. And he had the answer to his query.

It was in Miami, two seasons ago, when he'd been

down with Beaumonte for an unscheduled winter vacation. He had seen her in the expensive lobby of an expensive hotel, making her way on crutches. That was why he had remembered her, because she had been on crutches. That had stuck in his mind.

Smiling down at her he said suddenly, "Where were you on the night of December 15th two years ago? Don't huddle with your attorney. Let's have it without rehearsal."

"What do you mean?"

"Miami, wasn't it?"

"That's right." She watched him gravely. "How did you know?"

"I was there. I remembered you."

"Yes, I expect you would," she said.

His mind was working smoothly and sharply. Could she help him with Eddie? She looked smart; maybe she could pound sense into his head. The chance was well worth taking.

"I want to talk to you," he said. He smiled into her steady blue eyes and put his hands lightly over her bare shoulders. "I've got a proposition to make. Concerning Eddie, so don't haul off and slug me yet. How about having a drink with me when he's out safeguarding the ashcans in the neighborhood?"

"Let me go," she said quietly; but her voice was tight with anger. "Take your hands off me."

Carmody put his hands on his hips and studied her closely, bewildered by her reaction. "Take it easy," he said gently. "You're jumping to conclusions, I think."

"The Miami phase is over and done with," she said. "You'd better get that straight."

He didn't understand this. "I'm sorry you got the wrong idea," he said.

She was pale and defiant, but he saw that her lower lip was trembling. "Don't take it so hard," he said, still puzzled. "What can I say after I say I'm sorry?"

"You don't believe me, of course," she said.

"Why shouldn't I?"

"Stop grinning like an adolescent at a burlesque show," she said angrily.

"They whistled in my day," Carmody said. "But that was quite a spell back. You know you're awfully touchy. Does it worry your psychiatrist?"

"You're very funny. I'll bet you do imitations, too."

"Don't try to creep into my heart with flattery," Carmody said, smiling at her. "I know you just want to borrow my badge to give to some police dog."

She started to say something but Eddie came swinging down the room, grinning cheerfully, and she turned her back to Carmody and let Eddie take her arm.

"We've got to rush it up a little," he said, patting her hand. "You two have a chance to get acquainted?"

"We sure did," Carmody said, looking at Karen. He half expected her to tell Eddie about their little flare-up, but she avoided his eyes, said nothing. It would come later, he guessed. When she could flavor her version to Eddie's taste.

Outside they said their good-bys and Eddie and Karen walked away together in the soft clean darkness.

Carmody stared after them, frowning slightly and flipping the coin in his hand.

He would save Eddie all right. With or without help from this cool, poised little character. But probably with her help, he thought, smiling slightly.

She knew the score. She could count; all the way up to ten thousand.

He drove into the city on Broad Street and parked in a restricted zone on Fifteenth Street under the eye of a friendly traffic cop. Beaumonte was waiting for him but first he would have to check in with Lieutenant Wilson. There was always the need to preserve the illusion that he was a responsible member of the department.

Carmody called from a drug store. Wilson, a sharp and businesslike cop, sounded annoyed when he got through to him. "I can't run a shift without a sergeant, Mike," he said. "Where've you been?"

"Something developed on that Fairmount Park murder," Carmody said. "I'm meeting a character who wants to make a deal."

"Another Carmody exclusive," Wilson said dryly.

"Don't be sensitive. You can give it to the papers," Carmody said.

"I don't give a damn about that," Wilson said. "We've had two jobs tonight, a knifing in South with no leads and a murder in the Wagner Hotel. Everybody's out but me and I'm holding down your desk."

"I'll stop at the Wagner and take a look," Carmody said, checking his watch. The delay wouldn't improve Beaumonte's disposition, he knew. "Who'd you send on that one?"

"Dirksen and Myers."

"I'll take a look. And stop worrying."

"Gee, thanks," Wilson said. "It's real friendly of you to pitch in this way."

Carmody laughed and dropped the receiver back in place. He went out to his car and drove through center-city to the Wagner, a well-run commercial hotel near the railroad station. There he found Myers browbeating an hysterical little man in whose room the girl had been shot, and Dirksen talking baseball with a lab technician. The girl lay on the floor beside the rumpled bed, a heavily built blonde in her middle thirties. She wore only a slip and her make-up stood out like clown markings against the white emptiness of her face. Dirksen digressed reluctantly from the baseball to give him the story. The elevator operator had heard the shot and summoned the night manager, who had opened the room with his passkey. The girl was on the floor, a bullet hole under her heart, and the man, a furniture salesman from Michigan, was sprawled on the bed out cold.

"It was his gun fired the shot," Dirksen said in conclusion. "It's open and shut. He's playing dumb but he's our boy."

Carmody glanced around the room, frowning slightly. He noticed a tray of smeared highball glasses on the bureau with two whiskey bottles beside it. One was empty, the other full, and they were of different brands.

"What's our boy's name?" Carmody asked.

"Samuel T. Degget."

"Did you check his wallet? Was anything missing?"

"No, he's got all his money."

Carmody stared at Degget for a moment or so, trying to get an impression of the man. He was married and had grown daughters (Degget was telling Myers now in a high squealing voice). You couldn't be sure, Carmody thought, but he didn't seem to fit this kind of trouble. The girl, yes; the shooting, no. Degget looked like a cautious methodical person, and was probably a pillar of rectitude in his own community. When he cut loose it would be far from home and with all risks reduced to the absolute minimum. Everything bought and paid for, anonymous and artificial, and no unpleasant after effects except a big head in the morning. Why would he louse himself up with murder?

"What do you have on the girl?" he asked Dirksen.

"She works as a waitress in the coffee shop in the lobby. No folks in town. She lives in a boardinghouse on Elm Street with another girl. One of the waiters in the coffee shop remembers that Degget and she were pretty friendly. You know, he kidded around with her a lot."

Carmody frowned and looked once more at the whiskey bottles. Two different brands, one bottle empty, the other full. He checked his watch. The State liquor stores had closed two hours ago; he was wondering where Degget had got the second bottle. It wasn't likely that he had bought them both at the same time; if so, they would have been the same brand.

He glanced at Dirksen, who wet his lips. "Something wrong?" Dirksen asked, worried by Carmody's expression.

"Call the bell captain and ask him if there was any service to this room tonight," Carmody said.

Dirksen was on the phone a moment, and then looked over the receiver at Carmody. "No service, but somebody from here asked to see a bellhop.

"They may have run out of booze and wanted another bottle," Carmody said sharply. "Bellhops can find one for a price. Get the name of the boy who came up here, and find out if he's still on duty."

"Sure, sure." Dirksen looked up from the phone a moment later. "It was a fellow named Ernie, but he's not around. Do you think—"

"Get his address and send a car out there. And put him on the air. He can't be far away. Take Degget in as a material witness but get this guy Ernie."

"Right, Sarge." With routine to absorb him, Dirksen was crisp and confident. Myers drifted over, looking puzzled. "What's all this, Mike?"

"It was Jack the Ripper, really," Carmody said, smiling coldly at him. "I spotted it right away."

"What's funny about it?" Myers said, irritation tightening his cautious mouth.

"Nothing at all," Carmody said. "Actually, it's pretty sad."

"We got the man who—"

"No you haven't," Carmody said. "Not if my hunch is right. But Dirk can fill you in. I've got to be going."

It was nearly midnight when he got to Beaumonte's, and by then the night had turned clear and cool. Beaumonte opened the door and said, "Well, you and your brother must have had quite a talk." He wore a crimson silk dressing gown and held a pumpkin-sized brandy snifter in one hand.

"Sorry to keep you waiting," Carmody said. He strolled into the room and saw with a slight shock that Bill Ackerman was sitting in a deep chair beside the fireplace. The Delaney business was very big, he knew then. Nothing but high-priority operations could get Ackerman in from the country.

"Hello, Mike," Ackerman said, smiling briefly at him.

Carmody smiled and said hello. There was another man sitting in a chair with his back to the window, a powerfully built young man with wide pale features and dull observant eyes. Carmody said hello to him, too. His name was Johnny Stark and he had been a highly touted heavyweight contender until something went wrong with his ears. He was slightly deaf, and worrying about it had stamped a solemn, surprised look on his face. Ackerman owned his contract when he was fighting, and had taken him on as bodyguard when the medical examiners barred him from the ring. Stark sat with his huge hands hanging between his legs, his fairly good ear cocked toward Ackerman and his dull eyes flicking around the room like those of an inquisitive dog. He mumbled his answer to Carmody's greeting; this had become a habit since his hearing had gone bad. He was never sure what people said to him and he covered up with grunts and mumbles which could mean anything.

"Well, how'd it go?" Beaumonte said, easing himself into the sofa.

"The kid was sensible; he'll cooperate," Carmody said.

This wasn't a lie, he thought; he'd bring Eddie around some way.

"That's just fine," Beaumonte said, smiling at him. "I told you I didn't want trouble."

"There won't be any."

Ackerman stood and stretched leisurely, his hands stuck deep into his trouser pockets. Carmody didn't know whether he had been listening or not; it was impossible to guess accurately about anything connected with Bill Ackerman. He was a tall man in his middle fifties, with the lean, disciplined body of a professional soldier.

There was nothing to be learned from his features, which were tanned and hard, nor from his eyes which were merely sharp black globes beneath bushy gray eyebrows. His hair was the color of well-used and well-kept silver, and he dressed like a banker in town and a rancher in the country. He was a cold, controlled man who emanated a quality of blunt, explosive power; there was none of Beaumonte's phoniness in him. He lived in the country because he liked it there. The fact that it was pleasant for his wife and two daughters was simply coincidence. Had he wanted to live in the city, that's where he would live. Ackerman was driven by cool, dispassionate greed; he wanted to expand and expand, consolidate his gains and expand again. There was no definite goal on the horizon; it was the struggle as well as the victory that pleased him. Greed dominated his life. His farms and stock paid for themselves and his foreman and hands admired his shrewd tough efficiency. Everything in Ackerman's operations paid its way or was dropped. His world was money, and rivers of it flowed to him from handbooks and policy wheels throughout the state. More of it rolled in from his trucking and contracting firms, from fleets of cabs and packing houses. The money mounted faster and faster, and with a fraction of it he bought immunity from the law. Every cop he hired, every politician he subsidized, every judge he elevated became a prop to his empire, chained into place forever by guilt. No one got away from him; men were chattels, and he was as greedy for them as he was for money.

Carmody wasn't afraid of Ackerman; but he wondered why he bothered to tell himself this so often. If there was anyone to fear in this deal, it was Ackerman. He had fought his way up in the rackets with cold and awful efficiency; he had begun in Chicago with Dion O'Bannion's hoodlums, had run his own mob after repeal and had moved east to crash into the unions and the black market during the war. His past was marked with terror and violence but somehow he had come through it without being killed or jailed for life.

Now he stared at Carmody, his eyes narrowed under the bushy gray brows. "Your brother is a smart man, Mike. Runs in the family, I guess."

Carmody felt a sharp surge of anger at that. But he said quietly, "He's smart enough."

"Specifically, he won't identify Delaney at the trial. Is that right?"

"That's the agreement."

"What is it costing us?"

"Ten thousand. That's what Beaumonte said."

"It's a fair price," Ackerman said, rubbing his jaw. He

didn't like paying off; it wasn't natural for money to flow the other way. "Probably more dough than he's ever seen in one piece, eh?"

"Sure," Carmody said.

Ackerman said casually, "I want to talk to him, Mike. Fix it up for tomorrow night."

"Will that look good?" Carmody asked. He knew Ackerman had tried to jolt him, and that was ominous. It meant that Ackerman hadn't believed him completely. He smiled coldly, his tough strength and brains responding to the challenge. "If you're seen huddling with him before the trial it won't look good when he double-crosses the D.A."

"I said I want to talk to him," Ackerman said, watching Carmody curiously. He looked more surprised than angry. There was never any discussion about his orders; he insisted on automatic compliance. "You bring him here tomorrow night. Let's say ten o'clock. Got that?"

Beaumonte was watching them over the rim of his brandy snifter, and Johnny Stark had cocked his good ear anxiously toward the edge in Ackerman's voice. The tension held in the long graceful room until Carmody dismissed it with a little shrug. "Sure, I've got it. Ten o'clock."

"That's about all then, I guess," Ackerman said. "I'll see you, Mike."

"So long."

After he had gone Ackerman sat down and lit a cigar. When it was drawing well he glanced at Beaumonte through the ropey layers of smoke. "I don't know too much about Carmody," he said. "What kind of a guy is he?"

"He's tough," Beaumonte said, nodding. "But he's all right."

Ackerman said nothing more and Beaumonte became uneasy. He waved the heavy smoke away from his eyes, and said, "What's the matter? Don't you trust him?"

Ackerman used one of his rare smiles. "I'm like a guy in the banking business. I don't do business on trust. What's Carmody's job?"

"Just a job," Beaumonte said. "He keeps an eye on the bookies in West, does some collecting, checks the records of a guy who wants to open a horse room or run a policy game. That kind of thing. And he settles beefs. He's good at that."

Ackerman rubbed his smooth hard jaw and was silent again for several minutes. Then he said, "Well, we've got a beef. Think he's the man to settle it?"

"Well, that's up to you," Beaumonte said. Ackerman's manner was making him nervous. He liked straight, direct orders; but Ackerman wasn't giving orders. He was giving him an unwelcome responsibility in the deal. Beaumonte frowned, watching Ackerman hopefully for a crisp, final decision. In his heart he was a little bit afraid of Carmody; there was a look on the detective's face at times that made him uneasy.

"We'll give him a chance to settle it," Ackerman said tapping his cigar on the side of an ashtray. "But just one. I don't like the brother angle."

"Blood is thicker than water, eh?"

"That's it," Ackerman said, using another rare smile.

"But it's not thicker than money. Anyway, I'm going to hedge the bet just in case. You call Dominic Costello in Chicago and ask him to line us up someone who can do a fast job."

Beaumonte liked this much better. The decision was made, the orders given and he was in the clear. "I'll take care of it," he said. "How about a nightcap?"

"Okay. Make it light though, we're driving to the country tonight."

3

CARMODY DROVE directly across town to his hotel which was near the center of the city and about a block from the river. He parked a car length from the canopied entrance and told the doorman that he would be going out again shortly.

Carmody had lived here for six years, in a three-room suite on a premium floor high above the city's noise and dust. Letting himself in, he snapped on the lights and checked the time. Twelve-thirty. He had missed his shift completely, which would give Wilson something to complain about tomorrow. Let him, he thought. There was more at stake now than eight hours of routine duty.

First he had to get fixed on Karen Stephanson. She might be the lever to pry Eddie off the spot. Carmody paced the floor slowly, thinking over each word of their conversation, trying to recall every expression that had shifted across her small pale face. Finally, he sat down at the phone and called a man named Tony Anelli, a gambler who spent six months of each year in Miami.

Anelli sounded a little tight. "Howsa boy, howsa boy?" he said cheerfully. Carmody heard a woman's high laughter in the background.

"I'm looking for some information," Carmody said.

"Came to the right party," Anelli said. "We got a party going, as a matter of fact." This struck him as comical and he began to laugh. Carmody let him run down and then said, "Do you know anything about a girl named Karen Stephanson?"

"Karen Stephanson? Sounds Swedish," Anelli said. He was silent a few seconds. "It's familiar, Mike. I wish I wasn't loaded. The old head is turning around like a merry-go-round. Wait a second. I met her a couple of times, if she's the same dish. Thin girl, brown hair, kind of serious. Does that fit?"

"Yeah, that fits," Carmody said. "What do you know about her?"

"Well, nothing much. She was Danny Nimo's girl."

"Danny Nimo?"

"He ran a string of handbooks in New Orleans. Pretty rough character."

"She was his girl, eh?"

"Yeah, that's right. He's dead though. Died a year or so ago of pneumonia," Anelli said. "That's what always gets those big chesty guys. Let's see now. I met her in Miami in '50 or '51. She'd been in a hell of an accident. Nimo took me up to the hospital to see her, and that's why I remember her, I guess."

"What kind of an accident?" Carmody asked. He was thinking of her coldly and savagely. The pale little face, the poised and regal manner, and twisting his brother around in her slim hands like a piece of helpless clay. A bitter smile appeared at the corners of his mouth. He'd put an end to that act.

"It was an automobile accident," Anelli said. "Nimo was driving, and the story was that he was drunk. They hit a truck head-on; he told me her legs were broken in a dozen places."

In spite of his anger, Carmody winced. He hated the idea of physical suffering, not for himself but for others. It was about the only crack in his hard, iconoclastic shell. But her suffering was over, he thought, and now she was staging a cheap, phony act for Eddie. He understood her flare-up at his offer of a drink; she had thought he knew about her relationship with Nimo and was attempting to blackmail her into two-timing Eddie. A nice sweet kid. *The Miami phase is all over.* That's what she'd said. Sure, he thought, sure. Miami and Danny Nimo were a little trip along the primrose path, but now she was back on the strait and narrow, redeemed in the nick of time, saved by the bell, cheating the devil with a shoestring catch of her virtue. That would be her story, Carmody knew; told with a tactful tear or two and Eddie would buy it at any price.

"Thanks, Tony," he said into the phone. "See you around."

"Sure, keed. Take it easy. Wish I could do the same, but the night's going to be bumpy, I think."

Carmody hung up and walked into the bedroom, stripping off his suit coat. He showered and shaved, then opened the closet doors to choose his clothes. A dozen suits faced him in a neat row, and there was a line of glossy shoes with wooden blocks inside them in a rack on the floor. On either side of the suits were cedar-lined drawers filled with shirts, socks and underwear, and smaller trays containing cuff-links, tie-clips, handkerchiefs, a wallet and cigarette cases. Carmody took out a blue gabardine suit, a white shirt and a pair of cordovan shoes which had been shined and rubbed until they were nearly black. After dressing he glanced at himself in the full-length mirror. His thick blond hair was damp from the shower and there was an unpleasant little smile on his hard handsome face. All set for fun with Danny Nimo's ex-passion-flower, he thought. It should be good. He wondered what would happen to her when he dropped Danny Nimo's name into her lap. Fall apart in nice delicate pieces probably.

Carmody walked into the living room, made himself a light drink and put on an album of show tunes. She wound up her turn at two o'clock and Eddie had told him she lived at the Empire Hotel. Two-thirty should find her home, unless she was out with someone else. Staring at the gleaming sweep of the river, he realized he was letting himself get emotional about her. And that was no good. Anger could upset his judgment as drastically as any other passion. What he thought of her didn't matter; it wasn't his job to strip away her defenses. His only job was to make her help him with Eddie. So to hell with what he thought of her, to hell with everything but his dumb kid brother.

Still staring at the river, he lit a cigarette and sipped his drink. The music wrapped itself around him, filtering into his mind with stories of love—love lost, love found, love dying, love growing. Every kind of love there is, he thought irritably. The songs were as bad as the movie he had walked out of tonight. All promise, hope, and sickly enchantment. Did anyone know love as it was defined by these groaning singers? Where was this nostalgia, this grandeur, this thing that could enrich a man even as he lost or destroyed it?

Well, where was it? he asked himself. Not in this world, that was certain. It was like Santa Claus, and the big kind man with whiskers who looked down from the clouds with a sad smile on his face. Fairy tales for dopes who would fall on their faces if it weren't for these crutches.

To get his mind off it, he emptied an ashtray and straightened the pile of magazines on the coffee table. The room pleased him with its look of expensive comfort. It needed pictures, but he hadn't enough confidence in his own judgment to buy the modern paintings he thought he liked, and he balked at the hunting prints which a dealer had told him would go with just about anything. Glancing about, Carmody remembered the way his father had hung holy pictures around the house with a bland disregard for anything but his own taste. St. Michael with his foot on Lucifer's neck, the good and bad angels, St. Peter dressed like a Roman senator and St. Anthony looking like a tragic young poet. All over the place, staring at you solemnly when you snapped on the lights. Carmody hadn't minded the pictures as much as his father's stubborn insistence on sticking them in the most conspicuous spot in every room. It was like living in a church. Carmody hardly remembered his mother; she had died two months after having Eddie, when he himself was just eight years old. The old man had raised his sons alone; getting married again had never crossed his mind.

The stubborn old fool, Carmody was thinking, as he

got ready to leave. He'd been sure he had a strangle hold on happiness and eternal bliss. Everything was settled, all problems were solved in advance by his trust in God.

I'd like to see him handle this problem, he thought bitterly. The old man would tell Eddie not to worry, to make a novena and do what he thought was right. That would be great except for the fact that Ackerman and Beaumonte didn't believe in novenas. Prayers were a waste of breath in their league. The old man couldn't save Eddie with a lifetime on his knees. But I'll save him, Carmody thought. Without prayers. That's my kind of work.

The Empire was a quiet, respectable apartment hotel in the Northeast section of the city. Carmody got there at two-thirty, parked on the dark, tree-lined street and walked into the tiled lobby. He found her name printed in ink on a white card and rang the bell. There was a speaking tube beside the row of cards. She answered the third ring.

"Yes? Who is it?"

"This is Mike Carmody. I want to see you."

She hesitated a moment, then said coldly, "It's a bit late, don't you think?"

"Wait a minute. What's wrong with a friendly chat?"

"You don't see anything wrong with coming up here at two-thirty in the morning?"

"People will talk, eh?" he said dryly. "Well, that's okay. I don't mind."

"Please, Mike, you're dead wrong about me," she said, her voice changing.

"Save all that," he said. "This concerns Eddie. Now press the buzzer before I get mad."

"Is this how you get what you want?" she said. "By kicking people around?"

"Press that buzzer," Carmody said. "I'm not kidding, bright eyes. Your virtue, such as it is, won't get a work-out. Open up, damn it."

There was a short pause. Then the lock clicked sharply. Smiling slightly, he opened the door and walked down a short carpeted hallway to the elevator.

She was waiting for him at the doorway of her apartment, her small head lifted defiantly. She wore a blue silk robe and a ribbon held her hair back from the slim line of her throat. Without make-up her face was pale, but her steady blue eyes were bright and unafraid.

Carmody walked toward her, still smiling slightly. She would play this on a very high level, he guessed. All poise and dignity. She created an illusion of strength and dignity, but Carmody wasn't impressed. He had worked too long as a cop to be impressed by externals. Underneath that thin crust of confidence he knew there was nothing but guilt. What else could there be?

Smiling down at her, he said, "Thanks for letting me come up."

"I had no choice," she said shortly.

"That's a dull way to look at it."

She turned into her apartment and he followed her and tossed his hat into a chair. The living room was impersonal but comfortable; a TV set stood in one corner and a studio couch, made up now with sheets and blankets, was pulled out a few inches from the opposite wall. There were chairs, lamps, a coffee table with copies of *Variety* and *Billboard* on it, and a tall breakfront in which he saw shelves of dishes.

"Cosy," he said, nodding.

"You said you wanted to talk about Eddie."

"We'll get to him in a minute."

She shrugged lightly. "We'll do it your way, of course."

"That's right," he said.

"It's been a long day," she said. Her expression changed then, relieved by a tentative little smile. "Don't you have any soft spots? I'd be grateful if you'd make this brief and let me go to bed." She tilted her small head to one side. "How about it, Mike?"

"I'm covered with soft spots," Carmody said. "Sit down and be comfortable. This won't take long."

She moved to a chair and sat down slowly. The limp wasn't obvious; it was only suggested by the careful way she held her body—as if she were crossing a floor on which she had once taken a bad fall.

"What do you want?" she asked him.

Carmody sat down on a footstool in front of her, his big hands only a few inches from the folds of her robe. "Don't you want to guess?" he said.

"I expected you to be subtle about it," she said evenly, but a touch of color had come into her cheeks. "Flowers maybe, and a few kind words. But you've made this pretty cheap. Was that what you wanted?" Then she shook her head quickly and tried to soften his eyes with a smile. "You're wrong about me, Mike. What do I have to do to prove it?"

"Relax," Carmody said. "I'm here about Eddie. Listen

now: he had the bad luck to identify a murderer last month, and the guy is important. Has he told you anything about this?"

"No."

"Well, Eddie stumbled on a shooting. The murderer got away, but was picked up on his description. At the trial next month Eddie can send him to the chair. But that can't happen. Eddie's got to refuse to make the identification. Unless he agrees to that he's in bad trouble. Do you understand this?"

"Yes, I think so," she said slowly. The color had receded from her cheeks. "It's always the same, isn't it? Important people can't be bothered going to jail." She studied him with a fresh awareness. "And you're a friend of the important people?"

"One of their best friends," Carmody said. "But Eddie's my brother and I don't want him hurt. That's why I need your help."

"What can I do?"

"To start with, answer my questions. I know he's crazy about you. But how do you feel about him?"

"I like him a lot. He's good-natured, gentle, he's straight and dependable, and—"

"Okay, okay," Carmody said, cutting across her words impatiently. "I don't want a litany. Do you love the guy?"

"Not yet."

Carmody looked at her in silence, trying to keep a check on his temper. Who in hell was she to dilly-dally with his brother? To play the shy maiden with an honest guy like Eddie?

"What're you waiting for?" he asked her coldly. "Butterflies in your stomach and stars in your eyes?"

"What right have you got to be sarcastic about it?" she said, leaning forward tensely. "It's none of your business. You don't have any authority to barge in here and grill me about Eddie. I'm not a suspect in one of your cases."

"Now listen to me, bright eyes," Carmody said, standing suddenly, and forcing her back into the chair with the threat of his size and power. "I know who you are and what league you played in. As Eddie's brother that gives me plenty of rights." Staring down at her he saw the fear in her eyes, the guilt that lay beneath her crust of angry innocence.

"You were Danny Nimo's girl, right?" he said coldly.

"That's right."

"That's right. Is that all you've got to say?"

"What else is there to say?"

"Where's the rest of it? Didn't he hold the mortgage on the family estate? Wasn't he trying to lure your sister into the white slave racket? Where's the cute story of how you got mixed up with him?"

"There's no cute story," she said in a low voice. "No estate, no lily-pure sister. I liked him, that's all."

"That's all?" Carmody felt a thrust of anger snap his control. He caught her thin arms and jerked her to a standing position. "You had to have a reason," he said, his voice rising dangerously. "What was it?"

"Let me go. Take your hands off me," she cried, struggling impotently against the iron strength in his hands.

"Did you tell that to Danny Nimo? Did you tell him to take his hands off you?"

She was beginning to cry, her breath coming in rapid gasps. "Damn you, damn you," she sobbed. "Why are you doing this to me?"

Carmody shifted his grip and held her effortlessly against him with one arm. "Cut it out, bright eyes," he said. "There's no need for a big act. I know you, baby, we're the same kind of people, the same kind of dirt." With his free hand he forced her head back until their eyes met and held in a straining silence. "Now look," he said softly, "I'm going to use you to save Eddie. You'll do what I say, understand?"

"Let me go," she whispered.

"When you understand me, bright eyes." He studied her pale, frightened face, hating her pretence of maidenly fear and virtue. She acted as if his touch would contaminate her innocence. What gave her the right to that pose? He kissed her then deliberately and cruelly, forcing his mouth over hers and pulling her slim struggling body against his chest. For a moment he held her that way, locked tight against his big hard frame, knowing nothing but violence and anger and bitterness. And then, slowly, reluctantly, there was something else; her lips parted under his and the anger in him was replaced by a wild urgency. Carmody fought against its overwhelming demand and pushed her roughly away from him. They stared at each other, their breathing loud and rapid in the silence. "Does that prove it, bright eyes?" he said thickly. "Does that prove we're the same kind of people?"

She twisted her arms free and began to pound her small fists against his chest. "You can't say that, you can't say that," she cried at him.

Carmody took her arms and put her down in the chair. "Take it easy," he said, still breathing hard. "It's a little late to start fighting for your honor."

She turned away, avoiding his eyes, and struck the arm of the chair with the flat of her hand. "You pig, you animal," she said in a trembling voice. Tears started in her eyes and ran down her pale cheeks. "Why did you·do this? Have I ever hurt you? Am I so dirty you think you can wipe your feet on me?"

"Take it easy," he said again, running both hands through his hair. Her tears made him angry and uncomfortable. He hadn't meant to hurt her; in spite of his deep cynicism about people, he had held on to an old-fashioned idea that women should be treated gently. He waited until she got herself under control. Then he said, "You think I'm a heel. Well, okay. But if I'm rough it's because this is no Maypole dance we're in." He realized that he was apologizing obliquely to her and this puzzled him. "Look, I don't care if you and Eddie get married," he said. "That's none of my business. Maybe it will work out great. But you can't marry a body in a morgue."

"Will they kill him? Are they that important?"

"Yes, they're that important," he said. "So let's get serious. Supposing you told Eddie you needed money, a lot of it. Would he try to get it for you?"

"I don't know," she said, shaking her head slowly.

"We may have to find out," he said. Glancing down at her slim legs, Carmody lit a cigarette and frowned thoughtfully. Then he said, "Supposing you told him you needed eight or ten thousand dollars for an operation? A spinal operation, or a series of them, to keep you out of a wheel chair. It ties in with your accident logically enough. How about it? Would he try to raise the dough for you?"

"I don't know. I don't know," she said. "But I couldn't tell him that. I couldn't ask him to turn himself into a liar and a thief."

Carmody took a long drag on his cigarette, and watched her with narrowed eyes. "We can all do things we think we can't," he said quietly. "Does he know about Nimo?" When she refused to meet his eyes, he said, "I didn't think so. Would you like him to find out about that? And what happened here tonight?"

She shook her head wearily. "Don't tell him about that. He thinks everything of you. And of me. No, don't tell him, Mike."

"We've made a deal then," Carmody said. "I'll see him tomorrow and make one more pitch at him. If I can't wake him up, then it's your turn. You'll have to put the pressure on him for money. And the only way he can get it is by co-operating with me."

"He won't do it," she said. "He's too straight to do it."

Carmody looked at her appraisingly. "Don't worry about that. He can bend a little to keep you out of a wheel chair. Will you be here tomorrow afternoon?"

"I can be."

"I'll call you." Carmody paused to light a cigarette. "You've got everything straight now?"

"Yes. Won't you go?" she said in a low voice. "Won't you please leave me alone?"

"Okay, okay, I'm going," Carmody said. He pulled the door shut behind him and strode along the corridor to the elevator. A noise stopped him; he turned, listening again for the sound. It had been a small helpless cry, distinct and lonely, like that of someone in pain. But the silence of the building settled around him and he heard nothing but his own even breathing and the beat of his heart.

4

THE PHONE woke Carmody the next morning at nine-thirty. It was Lieutenant Wilson. "What happened to you last night?" he demanded.

Carmody raised himself on one elbow, completely alert; Wilson's tone warned him of trouble. "I told you, I was working on that Fairmount Park murder.

"Did you make any progress?"

"I've got a lead." Carmody frowned slightly; he didn't like lying to Wilson. They had gone through the police academy together and had been good friends for several years. Wilson was a straight, efficient cop, a family man with kids in school and a home in the new development at Spring Hill. He was everything that citizens expected their police officers to be, intelligent, fair and honest. Carmody wondered occasionally why Wilson still liked him; they were on opposite sides of the fence, and Wilson normally had no use for cops who drifted toward the easy buck.

"You got a lead, eh?" Wilson said. "Well, supposing you get in here and tell me about it. I'll give it to someone to run down."

"What's the big hurry?"

"Damn it, Mike, do I have to send you an engraved invitation when I want to talk to you? Get in here."

"Okay," Carmody said, glancing at the alarm clock.

He intended to see Eddie as soon as possible, and then, if necessary, Karen. "I'll be in at four o'clock," he said. "That's when my shift goes on."

"I want to see you now, right away," Wilson said.

"Okay, okay," Carmody said. He wasn't going in so there was no point in arguing about it. "How did that Wagner Hotel job turn out?"

"You struck gold, you lucky ape," Wilson said in an easier voice. "It was the bellhop, Ernie. Seems he brought a bottle up and found both Degget and the girl out cold. He was going through Degget's wallet when the girl woke and began to yell copper. He tried to talk her into a split, but she was too drunk to be sensible. Anyway, he got scared and shot her. He's put it all down on paper, so that winds that one up."

"The poor damn fool," Carmody said. "Why did he shoot her? You'd think a bellhop, of all people, would be smart enough to keep away from the big rap."

"He's not smart," Wilson said. "He's been in and out of trouble since he was a kid."

"This will be his last then," Carmody said. "How about the girl?"

"We got in touch with her mother. She's flying in to claim the body."

"It's a senseless mess all around," Carmody said. He glanced at his watch. "Well, get my name right for the papers."

"You're all right when you work at it," Wilson said. "I'll see you pretty soon, eh?"

"Sure." Carmody ordered his breakfast sent up, then showered, shaved and dressed. Eddie had worked twelve to eight and would still be asleep. Carmody decided to give him a few hours; he might be in a better mood if he had some rest. After coffee and orange juice he left his suite and drove across the city to the Midtown Club where he played three furious games of handball with a trainer. It was a punishing workout; the trainer had once been a semifinalist in the Nationals and he gave nothing away. Carmody was satisfied to win one of the three games and make a close fight of the other two. He baked out in the steam room afterwards and took an alcohol rub. Sitting in the dressing room later, a towel across his wide shoulders, he looked critically at himself in the mirror, noting the flat tight muscles of his stomach and the deep powerful arch of his chest. In good shape, he thought. The handball hadn't even winded him. Carmody's own strength and stamina had always surprised him slightly; his body simply ran on and on, meeting any demand he put on it, always more than equal to the occasion.

That's one thing I owe the old man, he thought; the indestructible constitution.

It was twelve-thirty when he left the club. He stopped at the Bervoort for cold roast beef with salad, then drank a bottle of cold beer and lit his first cigarette of the day. Relaxed and at ease, he sat for a few minutes at the table, savoring the fragrant smoke and the clean, toned-up feeling of his body.

Now he was ready for Eddie. This time he was sure of himself, charged with hard confidence.

The day was superb, clear and bright with sun. Carmody put the top of the convertible down before starting for the Northeast. He took the Parkway Drive, following the shining bend of the river, and enjoying the clean feel of the wind and sun against his face. Turning off at Summitt Road, he wound into the Northeast, driving through quiet residential streets where children played on the lawns, with their mothers coming to the porches occasionally to see that they weren't in trouble. This was Carmody's background; he had lived in this neighborhood until he was twenty-seven, increasingly bored by the middle-class monotony of the people, increasingly annoyed by the sharp but worried eye the old man kept on him. Our break was inevitable, he thought, turning into Eddie's block. We just split on the big things. But why couldn't people be reasonable about these disagreements? The old man was a fool, not because of what he believed but because he was so blindly insistent that he was right. You could argue with him up to a point; but beyond that there was no sympathy or compromise. Well, it's all over and done with now, Carmody thought, as he went up the wooden stairs of the old frame house and banged the old-fashioned brass knocker.

He waited, rapped again, then tried the door. It was open as usual. Carmody walked into the hallway, hung his hat automatically on the halltree and turned into the familiar shabby living room. Nothing much had changed in the seven years that he had been gone; the old man's outsized leather chair stood with its back to the windows, his piano was still stacked with Irish songs and church music and the dark, shadowy copy of Rafael's *Madonna* hung over the mantel, slightly crooked as always. The room was clean and he wondered if Eddie did the work himself. Very probably, he thought.

"Eddie?" he called. "You up yet?"

Eddie's voice sounded from the basement. "Hey, who's that?"

"Mike. Come on up."

"I've got to wash my hands. Sit down and make yourself at home."

Make yourself at home! Carmody glanced around with a wry little smile. There was no place in the world where that would be less possible. He couldn't be comfortable here; he felt smaller and less certain of himself in the old man's home. The memories of his father crowded around him, evoking all the past pain and friction. That was why he hadn't come back even after the old man died; he hated the uncertainty and guilt this shabby, middle-class room could produce in him. But it wasn't just the room, it was his father, Carmody knew. His feeling about the old man had started long before he had gone to work for Beaumonte, before he had learned that his job could be made to pay off like a rigged slot machine. It had begun with those arguments about right and wrong. To his father those words defined immutable categories of conduct, but to Carmody they were just words applied by men to suit their convenience. It was an emotional clash between a man of faith and a man of reason, in Carmody's mind. His father was a big, gentle, good-natured person, who believed like a trusting baby in the fables of his childhood. Like Eddie, for that matter. But you couldn't tell them different. It only hurt and angered them. Maybe that's why I feel guilty, he thought. It's the reaction to destroying anyone's dream, even if you're only showing up Santa Claus as the neighbor across the street with a pillow under his shirt and a dime-store beard on his chin.

Turning to the mantel, he picked up a dried-out baseball from a wooden saucer. He was remembering the game in which it had been used, as he tossed it up and down in his hand. The police department against the Phillies' bench. A big charity blowout. Carmody had tripled home the winning run in the bottom of the tenth inning. This was the ball he hit off a pitcher who was good enough to win thirteen games in the majors that season. Eight years ago! He was working for Beaumonte then, taking the easy money casually and without much reflection; it seemed like just another tribute to his superior brains and strength. But he couldn't fool his father about the source of the money. The old man saw the new convertible, the good clothes, the expensive vacations, and that was when the sharp, worried look had come into his eyes. The blowup came the night after the game in which Carmody had tripped home the winning run.

He had picked up a set of silverware by way of celebration, the kind they'd never been able to own, and when he walked in with it trouble had started. Carmody tossed the baseball up and down in his hand, frowning at his father's piano. The old man had been singing something from the Mass the choir was doing the coming Sunday. It had got on Carmody's nerves. He had said something about it as he unwrapped the silver, and that touched off their last row.

Somewhere in the middle of the argument the old man

had picked up the crate of silverware, walked to the door and had thrown it out into the street.

"And you can follow it, laddy me boy," he'd yelled in his big formidable voice. "No thief is going to sleep in my house."

That had done it. Carmody walked out and didn't see the old man until his funeral, a year later.

He heard Eddie on the basement stairs and quickly put the baseball back in the little wooden saucer. Eddie came in wearing a white T shirt and faded army suntan slacks. A lock of his hair was plastered damply against his forehead and his big forearms were streaked with sweat and dust. "Well, this is a surprise," he said, smiling slowly.

"You're up early."

"I had some work to do in the basement. How about a beer or something?"

"Sounds good."

"Sure, one won't hurt us," Eddie said. He went to the kitchen and returned in a few moments with two uncapped, frosted bottles of beer. Handing one to Carmody he tilted the other to his mouth and took a long swallow.

"That hits the spot," he said, shaking his head. "You working out this way today?"

"No, I'm here to see you," Carmody said, and watched the little frown that came on Eddie's face. "I told Ackerman and Beaumonte that you'd be sensible. They want to see you tonight at ten o'clock."

"You had no right to do that," Eddie said.

"Would you rather I sat back and let them blow your brains out?"

"Let me worry about that." Eddie looked badgered and harassed; a mixture of sadness and anger was nakedly apparent in his eyes. "I hate having you mixed up with those creeps," he said, almost shouting at Carmody. "I always have. You know that. But I don't want any part of them. Can you get that?"

"You should be grateful I work for them," Carmody said, holding onto his temper. "Do you think you'd get this break if you were some ordinary beat-tramping clown?"

"Grateful you work for them?" Eddie said slowly. "That's almost funny, Mike. Listen to me now. I always thought you were a great guy. Next to the old man, I suppose, you were the biggest thing in my life. I carried your bat home from games, I hung around Fourteenth Street when you were on traffic, watching you blow the whistle and wave your arms as if it was the most important thing anyone in the world could do."

"All kid brothers are that way," Carmody said.

"Then you had the blowup with the old man," Eddie went on, ignoring him. "I didn't understand it, he never talked about it, but it damn near tore me in two. Then I found out about it a little later when I was a rookie in the old Twenty-seventh. The cop whose locker was next to mine was talking about a guy who'd got into trouble for clipping a drunken driver for ten bucks. And he wound up by saying, 'Your brother's got the right idea, kid. Take it big, or don't take it at all.'" Eddie turned away and pounded a fist into his palm. "They had to pull me off him. I damn near killed him. Then I did some checking and you know where that led. I had to apologize to that cop, I had to say, 'You were dead right, my brother's a thief.'"

"You take things too seriously," Carmody said. "You sound like a recording of the old man."

"Is that bad?"

"No, hell no," Carmody said angrily. "It's great if you want to live in a dump like this and go through life being grateful to the gas company for a fifty-dollar-a-week job."

"That's all you saw, eh?" Eddie said in a soft, puzzled voice. "And you're supposed to be smart. The old man enjoyed his food, he slept a solid eight hours every night and when he died grown men and women cried for him. None of them had memories of him that weren't pretty good, one way or the other. They still miss him in the neighborhood. Those things are part of the picture, too, Mike, along with this dump as you call it, and the fifty-dollar-a-week job. But you never saw any of that, I suppose."

"Let's get off the old man," Carmody said shortly.

"You brought him up. You always do. You're still fighting him, if you want my guess."

"Well, I don't want your guesses," Carmody said. He knew he was making no progress, and this baffled and angered him. Why couldn't he sell this deal? Eddie stood up to facts as if they were knives Carmody was throwing at his father. That was why they came to the boiling point so quickly in any argument; in anything important the old man came between them. He was the symbol of their opposed values and Eddie was always fighting to defend him, fighting to prove the worth of what his brother had rejected. Carmody understood that now and he wondered bitterly how he could save him against those odds.

"Just listen to me calmly for a second," he said, drawing a deep breath. "Go along with Ackerman and Beaumonte. Tell them you won't identify Delaney. At the trial you can cross them and put the finger on him. They won't dare touch you then, the heat will be too big. Is there anything wrong with that?"

"You don't think so, obviously," Eddie said. He looked mad and disgusted. "You don't care about double-crossing them, eh?"

"I'm thinking about you," Carmody said, angered by Eddie's contempt. "Maybe I don't look very noble, but that's how the world is run." He had the disturbing thought that their roles had somehow become reversed; Eddie was calm and sure of himself, while he was getting more worried by the minute.

"Let's drop it," Eddie said flatly. "You couldn't change my mind in a million years. Now I've got to wash up. I'm meeting Father Ahearn at St. Pat's in fifteen minutes."

"More vespers?" Carmody asked sarcastically. He couldn't quite believe he had failed.

"No, it's a personal matter," Eddie said. He hesitated, then said in an even, impersonal voice: "I want to talk to him about Karen. She's not a Catholic and I'm going to find out where I stand."

"You'll marry her?"

"If she says the word."

"You're dumber than I thought," Carmody said, in a

hard, clipped voice. He knew he had taken a step that could never be retraced but he was too angry to care. "Look that merchandise over carefully before you buy it, kid."

Eddie stared at him, swallowing hard. Then he said, "Get out, Mike. While you're in one piece."

"Ask her about Danny Nimo," Carmody said coldly. "See what happens when you do, kid."

"She told me about Nimo," Eddie said quietly.

"I'll bet she made a sweet bedtime story out of it," Carmody said. But he was jarred; he'd been certain she wouldn't tell him about Nimo.

"She simply told me about it," Eddie said. "That's all. What you make of it depends on how you look at things. Everything in the world is twisted and dirty to you because you're always looking in a mirror."

"She's playing you for a fool," Carmody snapped. His anger had stripped away all his judgment; nothing mattered to him but blasting Eddie's ignorant trusting dream. "Ask her about me, about the scene we played last night. Maybe that will wake you up."

Eddie walked toward him slowly, his big fists swinging at his sides. There were tears in his eyes and his square face had twisted with anguish. "Get out, get out of here!" he cried in a trembling voice. He stopped two feet from Carmody and threw a sweeping roundhouse blow at his head.

He can't even fight, Carmody thought despairingly, as he stepped back and let the punch sail past him. Pushing Eddie away from him, he saw that he was crying, terribly and silently. Damn it, he thought, as a savage anger ran through him, why doesn't he pick up a chair and bust me wide open? Doesn't he even know that much?

Stepping in quickly, he snapped a right into his brother's stomach, knowing he had to end this fast. Eddie went down, doubling up with pain and working hard for each mouthful of air. He stared up at Carmody in helpless agony. "Don't go, let me fight you," he whispered.

Carmody looked away from him and wet his lips. "I didn't mean to hit you, kid," he said. "I was lying about Karen. Remember that."

"Don't leave, let me get up," Eddie said, working himself painfully to his knees.

Carmody couldn't look at him; but he couldn't look at anything else in the room either. The piano, the *Madonna*, his father's chair, they were all as mercilessly accusing as his brother's eyes. He strode out the front door and went quickly down the steps to his car. It was torn open now, he thought bitterly. Karen was his last chance. Eddie's last chance. He pulled up at the first drug store he came to, went in and rang her apartment. When she answered he said, "This is Mike Carmody. I've got to see you. Can I come up?"

"I'll meet you downstairs," she said after a short pause.

"Okay, ten minutes," he said. She didn't want him in her apartment again; he knew that from the tone of her voice. "Don't keep me waiting," he said, and hung up.

She was standing at the curb when he got to her hotel, looking slim and cool in a chocolate-colored dress and brown-and-white spectator pumps. Her hair was brushed back cleanly and the sun touched it here and there with tiny lights. She had style, he thought irrelevantly, as she crossed in front of the car. It showed in her well-cared for shoes and immaculate white gloves, in the way she held her head and shoulders. Phony or not, she looked like good people.

She slid in beside him, moving with the suggestion of tentative that was peculiar to her; that was the accident, he thought, glancing instinctively at her legs. What had Anelli said? A dozen breaks?

"We'll drive around," he said. "I just talked to Eddie and we wound up in a brawl."

"How did that happen?"

"It was about you." He headed for the river, frowning as he hunted for words. "You told him about Nimo, didn't you?"

"Yes, I told him," she said.

Carmody glanced angrily at her, then back to the road. "Why didn't you tell me that last night?"

"Would you have believed me?"

"I guess not," he said. What was he supposed to conclude from this? That she was playing it straight with Eddie? Or was she shrewd enough to know that he would be disarmed by a clean-breast approach?

When they reached the river he parked in a grassy, picnicking area. The water sparkled with sunlight and in the distance he could see the tall buildings of center-city, shrouded with mists of fog and smoke. It was a pleasant summer scene; a few boys were playing at the river bank and sparrows hopped along through the thick fragrant grass. Carmody twisted around in the seat and got out his cigarettes. "I made no impression on Eddie," he said. "So now it's your turn. But first I've got to tell you something. I told him about us." He went on hurriedly as she turned sharply on him, a touch of angry color appearing in her pale face. "Now listen to me; I told him to ask you about the scene we played last night. He took a swing at me and I had to hit him. Then I told him I'd been lying about you and me. Whether he believed me or not I don't know."

"You told him about us, and then you hit him?" She shook her head incredulously. "In God's name, why?"

"I had to," he said stubbornly.

"You had to! Who made you? Who forced you to?" She stared at him, her eyes blazing.

Carmody looked through the windshield at the city in the distance. Then he sighed heavily. "I don't know, it just happened," he said. "But I'm trying to save his life. I struck out, so it's up to you."

"What kind of threats will you use now?" she asked him bitterly. "He knows about Danny Nimo, and you told him about us. You don't have anything on me now. So what comes next? A session of arm-twisting? A gentle slapping around?"

"Unless you want him killed, you've got to help," Carmody said. Her words had stung him but he felt no anger at her, only a heavy dissatisfaction with himself. "Tell him you need ten thousand for an operation and you may save his life."

"Supposing it doesn't work," she said, watching him. "Then what will you do?"

"What can I do?"

"You're a detective, aren't you? Why don't you arrest them?"

"That's a pretty picture," he said, smiling ironically. "A pretty picture right out of a fairy tale. Will you see Eddie tonight?"

"Yes, at eight."

"Okay," Carmody said, switching on the ignition. "He leaves for the station around eleven-thirty, I guess. So I'll call you at twelve."

"All right," she said quietly.

"I'll drop you home. I've got to get to work."

"The nearest cab stand will do," she said. "Thanks, anyway."

"Okay," Carmody said, and rubbed his forehead tiredly. He wished this were over, with Eddie alive and Ackerman and Beaumonte satisfied with the way he'd handled it. He'd had no idea it would be so tough.

It was three o'clock when Carmody checked into Headquarters. He nodded to Dirksen and Abrams, who had come in early, and walked into Lieutenant Wilson's office.

Wilson glanced at him briefly. "Sit down, Mike," he said.

"Sorry I'm late," Carmody said, taking a chair and loosening his tie.

"What kept you? The Fairmount Park murder?"

"No, a personal matter." Carmody was becoming annoyed. Wilson was a short, powerfully built man with curly black hair and a set of belligerent, no-nonsense features. He seldom hounded Carmody because he knew there was no point in it. But now he was acting like a truant officer with a boy who'd been playing hooky.

"I said I wanted to see you this morning," he said, pushing aside a report. "Didn't that mean anything to you?"

"Frankly, not a hell of a lot," Carmody said. "I was off duty and I had some personal matters to take care of."

Wilson's face hardened as he left his desk and closed the door of his office. "You didn't see a paper this morning, I guess," he said looking down at Carmody.

"No. What's up?"

"Superintendent Shortall resigned. Because of his health."

Carmody started to smile and then he saw that Wilson was serious. He whistled softly. "Well, well," he said. There was nothing wrong with Shortall's health; he was sound as a hickory nut. The significant thing was that Shortall had been Ackerman's man. "Who'll get his job?" he asked Wilson.

"Somebody honest, I hope."

"You think that's likely?"

"Listen to me, Mike," Wilson said, sitting on the edge of his desk and studying Carmody with serious eyes. "I've known and liked you a long time. I don't understand why. Maybe it's because you were the best cop in the city for a half-a-dozen years. But, anyway, I'm giving you a tip; don't be a smart guy too long. There comes a time when a city values a bit of dumb, old-fashioned honesty."

Carmody lit a cigarette and flipped the match at the ashtray on Wilson's desk. "What's on your mind, Jim?"

"Just this; I'm tired of the fix, I'm tired of guys like you and Shortall. And if they put an honest man on top of this department I'm going to turn in an unfitness report on you."

"Why the advance warning?" Carmody said, smiling slightly.

Wilson's face was troubled. "I told you, damn it. I like you, Mike. And here's the rest of my deal. If you start right now being a full-time cop again, I'll forget that report."

Carmody was silent a moment, staring at the curl of smoke from his cigarette. It would be a relief, he thought, to have nothing on his mind but being a full-time cop. He knew that this edgy feeling had grown from his concern over Eddie, but that didn't help him to shake it; how could he relax while his brother was stubbornly asking for a ticket to the morgue?

"Think it over," Wilson said, watching Carmody's troubled face closely. "And remember this; the city's changing. Big defense plants have come into this town in the last few years, and the men running them pay a houseful of taxes. And they want value from them. Parks, schools, things like that. They don't want bookies and brothels and bars clipping their workers every week. Neither do the unions. And when you get the unions working with the men who run the companies you got a clout that can stand right up to Ackerman and Beaumonte. Look at Shortall. They made the Mayor can him. And they've got others on their list. You're a tough guy, but don't get in their way, Mike."

Carmody had heard rumors of this before, but he

hadn't been too concerned. He still wasn't, as a matter of fact. He had too abiding a faith in man's lack of goodness to believe in reform and regeneration. These things were cynical, expedient measures that people forgot all about when the baseball race got tight or the job of being good citizens became a bore.

"Just think it over," Wilson said. "But don't take too long about it."

"Okay, Jim, thanks."

Carmody went out to his desk and checked the day's work with Sergeant Klipperman who was going off duty. Everything was quiet; two manslaughters were pending and he sent Abrams and Dirksen out to wrap them up. Myers came in fifteen minutes late, walking fast and trying to look as if he'd been delayed by something important. Carmody glanced at the big clock beside the police speaker but said nothing. He settled in his chair and studied the reports on cases being handled by his shift.

Myers drifted over in his shirt sleeves and made some comment on the weather. Then he said, "That was pretty sharp guesswork on those whiskey bottles last night." He smiled cautiously, trying to analyze the brooding expression on Carmody's hard handsome face. "Dirk and I would have caught it, but you beat us to it, I got to admit that."

Yes, you've got to admit it, Carmody thought wearily. A frank generous admission that you're a dope makes everything just dandy. He started to say something sarcastic but changed his mind. Why jump on Myers? Why jump on anybody? "I came after you'd handled the routine," he said. "I had a better chance to look around."

"That's right, with the routine out of the way you can look around," Myers said, nodding. He sauntered away, looking relieved.

Carmody worked listlessly, almost hoping for a flurry of something to take his mind off Eddie. Finally, he left his desk and walked across the street to the drug store. He had to call Beaumonte and tell him Eddie couldn't keep the appointment with Ackerman. Putting it off any longer would only make matters worse.

Nancy Drake answered the phone and it took him a moment to get through her to Beaumonte. She was in a giggling, half-tight mood and insisted on telling him of some hilarious impropriety her dog had committed. Carmody listened impatiently, feeling the heat of the booth settling around him and aware that his temper was dangerously short.

"Great, hilarious," he said. "Funniest thing I've heard in the last two minutes. Now put Beaumonte on."

"We are in a most pleasant mood, I must say," she said with drunken dignity. Then she let out a little scream and giggled again. "Dan just whacked me on the tail. Would you do that to a girl, Mike? Come on, tell me."

Carmody swore softly and rubbed the back of his hand over his damp forehead. Then Beaumonte's soft rich voice was in his ear. "Mike, she had six brandy punches before breakfast, if you can believe it." He didn't sound angry, just tolerantly amused. "When she pickles herself for good I think I'll put her in a bottle over the mantel. Like a four-masted schooner, only she's missing a couple of masts."

Beaumonte had been drinking, too, Carmody guessed. "What's the deal on Shortall's resignation?"

"Where you phoning from?" Beaumonte said, after a short pause.

"A drug store."

"Oh. There's nothing to worry about, Mike. Ackerman will put a man in tomorrow probably. Is everything set for tonight, by the way? With your brother, I mean?"

"That's why I called," Carmody said. "He can't make it."

Beaumonte paused, and Carmody heard his long intake of breath. "This isn't good," Beaumonte said quietly.

"The kid had a date and wouldn't break it," Carmody said. "Should I put a gun in his back and march him up to your place?"

"Maybe that wouldn't have been a bad idea," Beaumonte said. "When can he make it?"

"Tomorrow night."

"Okay, I'll tell Ackerman. But he don't like being stood up."

"Don't worry, he'll be there tomorrow."

"I'm not worrying," Beaumonte said. "That's your job. Remember that, Mike."

When Carmody returned to the City Hall he saw Degget, the little man who'd been mixed up in the Wagner Hotel homicide, standing at the house sergeant's window, collecting his personal effects. Degget recognized him and smiled awkwardly. "Sarge, I know what you did for me," he said. "They had me down as a murderer until you came in."

"Well, it's all over now," Carmody said.

"No, it won't ever be over for me," Degget said, his small mouth twisting with embarrassment and pain. "You know how a small town is. They'll hold this over me and my family till we're in our graves. And I don't even know if my family will want me around any more. It was in the papers, you see. I wired my wife but she hasn't answered yet."

"These things blow over," Carmody said. He squeezed Degget's thin shoulder with his hand. "It won't last." Why should I give a good damn, he thought, watching Degget's worried hopeless eyes.

"Well, it's my goose that got cooked," Degget said. "And I asked for it." Then he said quickly, "Look, I want to show my appreciation for what you've done." He reached for his wallet but Carmody caught his arm. "Never mind," he said. "I don't want—" He paused, remembering Myers' invalid wife and young daughters. "I'll tell you what," he said. "If you want to buy someone a drink, buy one for Detective Myers. Leave something in an envelope with the house sergeant. He'll see that he gets it. And Myers can use it."

"I'll do that, I sure will," Degget said.

Carmody started for the stairs but stopped and looked back at Degget's doleful little figure. He winked at him and said, "Cheer up. The boys at home will think you're a hero."

"Well, they'll want all the details anyway," Degget said, smiling sheepishly.

The afternoon and evening wore on slowly. It was one of those nights when the city seemed to be inhabited by saints. But the inactivity irritated him because it gave him too much time to think. When his shift was finally over he was in a touchy, explosive mood. At his hotel he called the Fanfair and asked for Karen.

When she answered he said, "This is Mike. Did you talk to Eddie?"

"Yes—he's just gone." Against the background noise of the bar her voice was high and light.

"What happened?"

"I couldn't do it," she said. "I couldn't tell him I needed ten thousand dollars for an operation."

Carmody stared at the phone in his hand, his face hardening into cold bitter lines. "This is pretty," he said. "Did lying to him go against your principles?"

"No one has the right to put that kind of pressure on him. To force him to make that kind of decision."

"You sweet little fake," he said savagely. "You didn't have the right, eh? Well, do you have the right to let him get killed?"

"I begged him to take care of himself," she said, and he heard her voice break suddenly. "He said there was nothing to worry about. He said—"

"You missed your chance, baby."

"Then don't miss yours," she cried at him.

"What do you mean? Listen—"

The phone clicked in his ear. Carmody stared at the receiver a moment, then slammed it down in the cradle. She was checking out. The act was over; Danny Nimo's girl knew when it was time to switch roles. But with his anger there was a cynical respect for her; she was looking after Number One, and that was playing it smart.

Carmody crossed the room to the windows and stared

out at the scene spreading below him; the river was shining palely and the high buildings loomed massively against the sky, their lighted windows forming irregular designs in the darkness. Eddie is my job, he thought, I was a fool to think anyone else cared a damn whether he lived or died.

5

CARMODY SLEPT uneasily that night and was up early in the morning. One thing had occurred to him by then: Why were Ackerman and Beaumonte worried about Delaney? This was something he should have checked immediately, and he realized that his emotional concern over Eddie was ruining his cop-wise judgment. What had Beaumonte said? That if Delaney talked it would cause trouble. But for whom? Ackerman or Beaumonte?

Carmody sat down at the phone, a cigarette between his lips, and began a cautious check on Delaney. He talked with two Magistrates, a Judge and half-a-dozen bookies, trying to learn something from casual gossip. The word was around, he soon realized; they knew Delaney was threatening to sing and that the big boys were worried. But no one cared to speculate on the nature of Delaney's information. Carmody gave it up after a while, but he wasn't discouraged. The clue might be in Delaney's past; Delaney had been a muscle boy in the organization when Ackerman and Beaumonte were on-the-make hoodlums instead of semirespectable public figures. That would be the angle to check.

Delaney's evidence must be something tangible and conclusive; otherwise, his threats to sing wouldn't bother Beaumonte and Ackerman. The job was to find that evidence and destroy it; that would pull Delaney's stinger, take the pressure off the big boys and leave Eddie in the clear. It wasn't a simple job and it had to be done quickly, but Carmody wasn't worried; he knew how to handle this kind of work. The city couldn't keep any secrets from him; he had studied it too long for that. A map of the city blazed in his mind; he knew the look of a thousand intersections and could reel off the houses and shops on each corner as easily as he could the alphabet. He knew politicians from the Mayor down to precinct drifters, and he understood the intricate balancings and give-and-take of the city's administration. The brothels and bars, the clubs and cliques, the little blondes and brunettes tucked away in handsome apartments in center-city, guys on the make, on the skids, on the way up— Carmody had them all indexed and cross-indexed in his formidable memory.

No, finding Delaney's source of pressure wouldn't be impossible, he thought.

Carmody went into the bathroom to shower and when he came out the phone was ringing. He picked it up and said, "Yes?"

"This is Beaumonte, Mike. Can you get over here around four? Ackerman wants to see you."

"Four? Sure, that's okay," Carmody said easily. He stood with his feet wide apart, a towel around his middle feeling the drops of water drying on his big hard shoulders. "What's on his mind?" he asked. "My brother?" It was a stupid, dangerous question, but he had to know.

"Some friend of his wants to open a handbook in West," Beaumonte said. "Ackerman wants you to take good care of him."

"Sure, sure," Carmody said, releasing his breath slowly. "Four o'clock then."

"Right, Mike."

Carmody went out to lunch and got back to his hotel at three o'clock. He washed his hands and face, changed into a dark-gray flannel suit and was on his way to the door when the phone stopped him. A high-pitched irritable voice blasted into his ear when he raised the receiver. "Mike Carmody? Is that you, boy?"

"That's right. Who's this?"

"Father Ahearn. I want to see you."

"I'm just on my way out, Father," he said.

"I'm down in the lobby. This won't take long."

Carmody checked his watch and frowned. "Okay, I'll be down. But I'm in a hurry."

"I'll be waiting at the elevator so don't try sneaking past me."

Carmody hung up, finding a grim humor in the situation. The old priest acted as if he were talking to one of his altar boys.

When the elevator doors opened Carmody saw that the last eight years had been hard on the old priest. At his father's funeral, which was the last time Carmody had seen him, Father Ahearn had been lively and vigorous, a tall man with gray hair and alert flashing eyes. But now he was slightly stooped and the tremors of age were noticeable in his heavily-knuckled hands. His hair had turned almost white but his eyes hadn't changed at all; they still flashed fiercely above the bold strong nose. He looked incongruous in the smart glitter of the lobby, a tired, bent old man in a black suit which had turned a grayish-green with age.

Carmody shook hands with him and suggested they take a seat at the side of the lobby.

"You want to go off and hide, eh?" Father Ahearn said.

You never manage him, Carmody remembered. "What's on your mind?" he said, edging him tactfully out of the traffic flowing toward the elevators.

"What's the trouble with you and Eddie?"

"That's a personal matter, Father."

"None of my business, eh? Well, when one brother strikes another in my parish I make it my business."

"Eddie told you I hit him?"

"Yes. I could see he'd been hurt. But that's all he would tell me." The old priest tilted his head and studied Carmody with his fierce eyes. "What was it? The girl?"

"I suppose you could say that."

"And what makes it any of your business?"

"I'm his brother."

"Ah," the old priest said softly. "His brother, is it? His keeper, you are. Isn't that a new role for you, Mike?"

Carmody felt embarrassed and irritated. "Look, there's no point talking about it," he said. "What's between me and Eddie doesn't concern you or the church."

"Now you listen to me, boy. I don't—"

But Carmody cut him off. "It's no use, I've got to be going, Father." He didn't like doing this to the old man and he hated the hurt look his words brought into his eyes; Father Ahearn had been a family friend for years, and had done them a thousand favors. He had got him summer jobs, had sent him to college on an athletic scholarship and had seen that Eddie stuck out his last year of school after the old man died. But that was long, long ago, in time and in values; it belonged to another world.

"All right, I'll not keep you," Father Ahearn said.

"I'll get you a cab."

"Never mind, you go on about your important affairs. But don't interfere with Eddie and his girl."

"You've met her, I guess?"

"What have you got against her?"

She's fooled him, Carmody thought. Probably had a cup of tea with him and smiled at his Irish stories. "There's no point going into it," he said.

"Very well. Good-by, Mike." The old man walked away, threading through the group of expensively dressed men and women. Carmody watched him until he disappeared, and there was a small, unhappy frown on his hard face . . .

He got to Beaumonte's at ten of four and found Nancy alone in the long elegant drawing-room. She wore a black dress with a full flaring skirt and junk bracelets on her wrists.

"Where's everybody?" Carmody asked her.

"Everybody? Don't I count?"

"I mean Ackerman and Beaumonte."

"Are they everybody?" she asked, smiling at him, her eyes wide and thoughtful.

"No, you count, too," he said.

"Sometimes it seems like they're everybody," she said, sighing sadly. There was a comic quality to her gravity; with her swept-up blonde hair, jingling bracelets, she was hard to take seriously.

"Don't get deep now," he said.

"You're like them, in a way."

"That's a compliment, I hope."

"You wouldn't care whether it was or not." A frown gathered on her smooth childishly round forehead. "That's what frightens me about all of you. You just don't care. Not like other people do. Everything in the world is just to use. A girl, a car, a drink, they're all the same."

"What got you into this mood?" he asked her.

"Too many drinks, I guess. That's Dan's analysis for all my problems." She put an expression of mock sternness on her face and pointed a finger accusingly at Carmody. "'You're a lush, you lush.'" Relaxing and sighing, she said, "That's his daily sermon. It's supposed to fix everything up dandy."

Carmody was touched by the unhappiness in her face. "You shouldn't worry so much," he said. He wondered why she stuck with Beaumonte. The same reason I do, he thought. The money, the excitement of being on intimate terms with power and privilege. Weren't those good reasons?

"The trouble is I don't feel like a girl any more," she said, making a studied pirouette on one small foot.

"Well, what do you feel like?"

"Like a faucet," she said, making a faster turn on her other foot. Her skirt flared out from her beautifully shaped, silken legs. "Look, I can dance. I'm a faucet," she said again, continuing the pirouettes. "Something Dan turns on and off, on and off. Whenever he wants to. Don't I dance gorgeously?"

"Just great."

She stopped spinning and looked at him, her eyes bright and excited. "I love to dance. Even when it was my work I loved it. Mike, how about taking me on a picnic some day?"

Carmody laughed. "Sure. We could stage it on the roof and have it catered by the Park Club. What gave you that idea?"

"No, the Park Club won't do," she said, sighing. "They'd send over ants in little tiny cellophane packages to give it a realistic touch. Excuse me. We need ice. Then I'll make us a couple of unwise drinks."

"Never mind me."

She looked at him thoughtfully. "How come you don't drink. I mean, get blind and drunk like the rest of us."

"I guess I don't want to be anyone else," Carmody said. "That's why people get drunk, I imagine. To forget what they are."

"That's a gloomy idea," she said. "It kind of hurts, too. Well, to hell with it. I'll get the ice and be somebody else. Maybe an ant at a picnic, who knows?"

A moment after she'd gone a key sounded in the front door and Beaumonte walked in, followed by Bill Ackerman and his huge watchdog, Johnny Stark, the ex-heavyweight. Something in their manner warned Carmody; Beaumonte, massive and immaculate in a white silk suit, looked sullen, and even Ackerman, who normally gave nothing away, was frowning slightly. Johnny Stark walked past Carmody and sat down in a straight chair with his back to the terrace windows. He flicked his eyes around the room but kept his good ear cocked toward Ackerman like a wary dog.

"More bum tips?" Carmody asked Beaumonte.

"We weren't at the track." Beaumonte stared bluntly at him, his eyes narrowed and unfriendly. "I've got more to do than sit on my tail in the clubhouse."

"I know you've got it rough," Carmody grinned.

"Don't be a comic. I'm in no mood for jokes."

"I worry a lot about your moods," Carmody said easily. "Sometimes they keep me awake all of five or ten minutes."

The silence stretched out as Beaumonte walked to the coffee table, picked up a cigar and faced him from the fireplace. This put Carmody in the middle of a triangle, with Ackerman standing before him, Beaumonte at his side, and Johnny Stark at his back. A faint warning stirred in him. Trouble was coming; he could sense it in their deliberate manner and hard watchful eyes.

"I expected to see your brother last night," Ackerman said. He was in a businesslike mood, his eyes frowning and black, his even features set in a closed, unrevealing expression. "What happened?"

"I explained that to Beaumonte."

"Explain it to me," Ackerman said coldly.

"My brother had a date and wouldn't break it."

"You're sure he hasn't changed his mind?"

"Of course not," Carmody said.

Ackerman smiled faintly but it didn't relieve the expression about his eyes. "I wanted to hear you say that, Mike." He glanced at Beaumonte. "There it is," he said.

"Yeah, there it is," Beaumonte said.

Ackerman opened his mouth but before he could speak Nancy came bouncing into the room, carrying a drink in one hand and humming a song under her breath. "Hello, Danny boy," she said, and skipped toward him with a series of intricate little steps. "I was dancing for Mike. He thinks I've got talent. Don't you Mike?"

Beaumonte swore violently at her and pulled the glass from her hand. Liquor splashed on the front of her skirt and over the tips of her black velvet pumps. She backed away, staring at him guiltily. Her face was white and her hands came together nervously over her breasts. "Why did you do that, Dan?" she asked in a small voice.

"Dancing! You've also been swilling my liquor like a pig."

"You said it was all right today."

"And now I'm telling you different," Beaumonte said, and hurled the glass across the room. It struck the wall beside one of his oils and shattered noisily. "I'll kick you back to the gutter if you can't stop acting like a rumhead." He caught her arm and shoved her toward the wide doors of the dining room. "Get out of here and sleep it off, you hear?"

"Don't shout at me, please Dan," she said, regaining her balance. "I'll go, please."

Carmody said softly, "Your manners stink, Beaumonte. Why don't you try to match them up with your paintings and imported wines?"

"Keep out of this, Mike," Beaumonte said, staring at him with hot furious eyes.

"Everybody relax," Ackerman said, and the words fell ominously across the silence. Johnny Stark came quickly to his feet and moved in on the group, responding like a dog to Ackerman's tone. Nancy backed slowly to the bar as Beaumonte mopped his red face with a handkerchief. "Okay, we're relaxed," he said, breathing deeply and staring at Ackerman. "Let's get this over with."

"Okay," Ackerman said, in the same dangerous voice. He swung around on Carmody. "You've lied to us. You made no deal with your brother. We talked to him this afternoon and he threatened to arrest us if we didn't clear out of his house. Got anything to say to this, you smart bastard?"

"I was working on him," Carmody said slowly. Talking would help nothing; they had him cold. But he went on, anyway, stalling for time. "He didn't like the idea, but I was softening him up. I could have brought him around."

"You lied to us," Ackerman said. "You were crossing me up, Mike. There's a lot at stake in this deal but you couldn't take orders. Well, I got no room around me for guys like you. You beat it now, and beat it fast."

"You aren't talking to a bellhop," Carmody said. He didn't know where this was heading and he didn't care. "I don't come and go when you press a button."

"You'd better listen when I press a button," Ackerman said. "We've got a file on you a foot high. When it goes to the Superintendent you go to jail. Keep that in mind, bellhop."

It's a bluff, Carmody thought, watching Ackerman. But he knew he was kidding himself. Ackerman never bluffed; he had a leash on every man who worked for him. It was the fundamental rule of his operations.

"I don't trust anybody," Ackerman said, as if reading his thoughts. "And least of all the cops who work for me. You've already sold yourself once when you start using your badges as collection plates. And you'll sell me out if I give you the chance."

"Let's go, Mike," Johnny Stark said, moving toward him with his slow, flat-footed walk. "You heard Mr. Ackerman."

"Okay," Carmody said, looking about the room, letting his eyes touch Ackerman and Beaumonte. "I'll run along." He picked up his hat from the chair and walked to the door, feeling the silence behind him and aware of their looks on his back. With his hand on the knob he paused a second. He was alone now, cut off from everyone. There would be no help from any quarter; Karen, Ackerman, Father Ahearn, even Eddie himself, they were all ranged against him, watching his futile efforts with contempt. But I've always been alone, he thought, as a gentle, pleasurable anger began to stir in him; he had thrown away the hollow props of faith and family because he had to stand alone. Turning his head slightly he caught Ackerman with his cold gray eyes. "What about my brother?" he said.

"We'll take care of that," Ackerman said.

Carmody let his hand fall from the knob. For an instant he stood perfectly still, his big body relaxed and at ease. Then he turned and walked slowly back into the room. "What does that mean, Ackerman?" he said quietly.

"Don't make a big mistake now," Ackerman said. "Just beat it. I'm tired of talk."

They can't push me this last step, Carmody thought. I'm a crooked cop with thieves' money in my pocket, but I won't look the other way while they murder Eddie. Drawing a deep breath, he felt nothing but relief at reaching a line he wouldn't cross.

"There'll be just a little more talk," he said coldly to Ackerman. "And you'd better listen good. Nothing happens to my brother. Get that straight."

Ackerman looked at Johnny Stark and said irritably, "Take him out of here."

"What?" Johnny asked him anxiously.

"Get him out, you deaf ape," Ackerman yelled. "You think I want lip from a stupid flatfoot."

"I told you to listen good," Carmody said, and the hard bright anger in his face brought a nervous slack to Beaumonte's lips. Johnny was moving in on him, his massive chin pulled down into his neck, but Carmody kept his eyes on Ackerman. "Nothing happens to my brother. Figure out some other way to get off the hook."

"I heard you," Ackerman said. "I've listened to loud mouths like you before."

"Not like me, you haven't," Carmody said gently. "Remember that." Then he laughed and swung around to face Johnny Stark, his eyes alive with fury. "Now throw me out, sonny boy," he said. "Earn your dough."

"Mike, you and me don't want to fight," Johnny said.

"Why not? That's what you're paid for."

Johnny hesitated, a sheepish smile touching his wide pale face. Without taking his eyes from Carmody, he said, "Mr. Ackerman, Mike carries a gun."

"Don't let that worry you," Carmody said. He took

the gun from his shoulder holster and flipped it suddenly to Johnny. "Now you've got one." While Johnny was turning it around gingerly in his massive hands, Carmody stepped in and hit him with a right that knocked him sprawling across the coffee table and into the fireplace.

Ackerman and Beaumonte scrambled aside, and at the bar Nancy screamed softly and put her hands to her mouth.

Johnny wiped his bleeding lips with the coat sleeve as he got slowly and purposefully to his feet. His little eyes were mean and hot. "You shouldn't have done that, Mike," he said, mumbling the words through split lips. "Now I'm going to hurt you."

"Come on, sonny," Carmody said, waiting for him with his hands on his hips. "You're no street fighter. I'll give you a lesson for free."

Johnny didn't answer. He came in fast, hooked a left into Carmody's side and tried for his jaw with an explosive right. It missed by half an inch but he recovered instantly and crowded Carmody back toward the wall with a flurry of punches that came out like pistons from his heavy shoulders. Carmody took a blow in the stomach and another that loosened a front tooth and sent a spurt of blood down his chin. Then he erupted; he could have handled it from a distance, cutting Johnny to pieces with his left, but that wouldn't have appeased his wild, destructive rage. He battered his way back to the middle of the room, trading punches with savage joy; he didn't want to do this the smart way, he wanted to be hurt, he wanted to be punished.

They stood toe-to-toe for half a minute, slugging desperately, and then Johnny broke it off and backed away, his breath coming in sharp whistles through his flat nose. He was cut badly around the mouth and there was a look of cautious respect in his narrowed eyes.

"Ackerman fixed your fights," Carmody said, grinning. "Didn't they ever tell you that."

Johnny leaped at him, swearing, and Carmody stepped back and let a punch sail past his head. Moving in fast he speared Johnny with a left and caught him off balance with a tremendous right that drove him across the room. Johnny bore back recklessly, but the right had weakened him; his breath was coming hard and he was down flat on his feet. Carmody hit him with another right and when it landed he knew the fight was over; the blow smashed into Johnny's throat and spun him around and down to the floor. Johnny screamed once in a desperate choking voice and his legs threshed as he fought to squeeze air into his lungs. He got enough down to quell his panic and then lay perfectly still, concentrating his strength on the painful work of breathing.

Carmody picked up his revolver, put it away in his holster and looked at Ackerman, his big chest rising and falling rapidly. "Remember what I told you," he said. "Nothing happens to my brother."

Ackerman smiled very carefully. The ingredients of death were in the room, he knew, and another jar might explode them in his face. "Maybe we can figure out something else," he said.

Beaumonte cried suddenly, "We don't want to hurt

him, but the crazy bastard hasn't got the brains of a two-year-old."

He had used the wrong word and he knew it instantly. Carmody walked toward him and Beaumonte said, "Now look," but that was all he got out; Carmody snapped a left up into his big padded stomach and Beaumonte's mouth closed on a sharp, disbelieving cry of pain. He sank to the floor slowly, settling like a punctured balloon, his face flushed with anguish and fear.

"It was just a manner of speaking," Ackerman said, still smiling carefully.

"It's a manner I don't like," Carmody said.

Nancy laughed suddenly, like a happy, delighted child, and skipped over to sit beside Beaumonte. She crossed her legs, spread her skirt out prettily then leaned forward and smiled into his crimson face.

"Daddy got a tummy ache?" she asked him merrily. "Or is Daddy over his ration?" Beaumonte stared furiously at her, his face squeezed with pain, his mouth opening and closing soundlessly. "Look, it's sloshing in the scuppers," she cried, and raised her glass ceremoniously and poured the contents over his head. "See it slosh, Daddy? And what the hell are scuppers, anyway? I've always meant to ask."

The liquor darkened the shoulders and lapels of his white silk suit and dripped down onto his lap, but he paid no attention to it. He sat awkwardly, hunched over like a Buddha, staring at her with murderous eyes.

Ackerman smiled at Carmody. "There's still time to settle our problem smartly."

"The time ran out," Carmody said, moving toward

the door but keeping his eyes on everyone in the room. "Remember what I told you, Ackerman. The guy you send after my brother has got to come through me first. He won't like that, I promise."

Ackerman shrugged slightly, and Carmody knew the break was clean and final. When he stepped from this room he wouldn't have a friend in the city. Okay, I don't need friends, he thought. I'm enough by myself, I'm Mike Carmody.

With a cold smile on his lips he turned and walked out the door.

Ackerman stood quietly for several seconds, frowning thoughtfully at the wall. Then, without looking around, he said, "Dan, did you get everything set with Dominic Costello?"

"He sent us a guy," Beaumonte said, his voice small and hoarse. "He's already on young Carmody's tail."

"Tell him to go to work," Ackerman said. "And you'd better figure out something to keep Carmody out of the way. Nobody will have a chance to get at his brother while he's around." His voice was flat and disgusted.

"Okay." Beaumonte still sat on the floor, watching Nancy. She smiled unsteadily at him as a slow fear began to work through her drunkenness. "I didn't mean it," she said in a sad, little girl's voice. "Honest, Dan."

Ackerman looked around then, his eyes dark and furious. "Maybe you can handle my business better than you handle your women," he said to Beaumonte. "You'd better, that's all I can tell you."

Johnny Stark climbed slowly to his feet, massaging his neck with both hands. "He caught me in the windpipe, Mr. Ackerman," he said in a squeaking voice. "I'd of got him if he hadn't caught my windpipe."

"You couldn't take him with an armored tank," Ackerman said, glaring at him. "What do I pay you for? To listen to birds singing?" Turning abruptly he walked to the door. Over his shoulder he said, "Don't bother coming along, Stark. I'm safer alone." He walked out and slammed the door shut behind him with a crash.

"Give me a hand, Johnny," Beaumonte said.

"Sure, sure," Johnny said quickly, glad to be useful to someone. He got behind Beaumonte, put both hands under his armpits and hauled him to his feet. Beaumonte swayed and put his hand for support against the mantel. "He could have killed me," he muttered. "He could have broke something inside me."

"Yeah, he can hit," Johnny said, nodding earnestly.

Nancy put a hand timidly on Beaumonte's forearm. "Look at me, Dan." She was pale and trembling, sobered by her fear. "It was just a joke. You do things like that to me sometimes, don't you? I was drinking too much, like you said. But I'm going on the wagon, I promise, Dan."

Beaumonte turned away from her, pulling his hand free from her arm. "You're going back where I found you," he said slowly.

"Dan, please!" She tried to turn him around but he shook her off with a twist of his big round shoulders. "Please, Dan! It was just a crazy joke," she said, beginning to weep.

"Johnny, you know where Fanzo's place is?" Beaumonte said to Stark.

"Yeah, sure, Mr. Beaumonte."

Beaumonte drew a deep breath. "Take Nancy there, take her if you have to break her legs and carry her," he said, in a slow empty voice. "You got that? I'll phone him so he'll have the welcome mat out."

"Dan, what are you going to do to me?" Nancy cried, backing away from the two men. She brought her hands to her mouth and the bracelets on her wrists jangled noisily in the silent room.

Beaumonte looked at her then for the first time since he'd got to his feet. "Why did you do a thing like that with Ackerman watching," he said thickly.

"I told you it was just a crazy gag."

"I'm going to pay you off good," he said. "You got no more loyalty in you than a stick of wood."

"Dan!" she cried softly, as Johnny Stark put a massive hand on her wrist. Her eyes were wild and unbelieving. "You aren't going to do this to me. It's a joke, I know. Tell me it's a joke, Dan."

"Get her out," Beaumonte cried. "Get her out of here."

When they were gone, Beaumonte drew a deep ragged breath and began to walk about in small aimless circles. Finally, he stopped and went quickly to the bar. He made himself a brandy and soda, slopping the ingredients into the glass, and then sat down in a deep chair and stared at the long silent room. For several minutes he remained motionless, his body slumping forward slightly, and then he moaned deep in his throat and began to pound his fist slowly against his forehead. But the sound of her weeping stayed loud in his mind.

6

CARMODY DROVE directly to his hotel, recklessly ignoring lights and traffic. It wasn't quite six yet, but he knew that Ackerman would plan and act swiftly. The order might already be out, and that meant he had to find Eddie fast. But a dozen phone calls to his home, his district and his favorite bars, failed to turn up a lead.

Carmody rang Karen's apartment and drummed his fingers on the table as the phone buzzed in his ear. Then the connection was made, and she said, "Hello?"

"Karen, this is Mike. Have you seen Eddie today?"

"No. . . . What's the matter?"

"If you see him, tell him to call me at my hotel. Will you do that? I couldn't stall the big boys any longer. Tell him that, too."

"Does that mean trouble?"

"Not for you, bright eyes. But it does for Eddie. If he calls you—"

The phone clicked dead. For a moment Carmody sat perfectly still and then he swept the receiver off the table. She was staying in the clear. There was trouble coming and Danny Nimo's girl would take a warm bath, do her nails and keep nicely out of it. Well, what had he expected?

But underneath his anger there was a growing fear. He shouldn't have tipped his hand to Ackerman; that spotted them a big advantage. Where in hell were his brains?

He needed help in finding his brother but he didn't know where to turn. Anyone who knew this was Ackerman's business would want no part of it. The men on his shift were his only bet, but it wouldn't be easy to find them; his shift had started its three-day relief that morning and they might be out of town or visiting relatives. Some damn thing. Carmody tried Dirksen first, because he was the dumbest, but got no answer. Abrams' daughter talked to him and said that her daddy had gone to the shore to do some fishing. Carmody thanked her and hung up. That left Myers. He put through the call.

Myers sounded as if he had been sleeping. "Hi, Mike. What's up?" he said.

"I need some help. My brother's in a little trouble and I've got to locate him. But I need a hand. How about it?"

"In a little trouble, eh?" Myers said cautiously.

"That's right. Look, he lives on Sycamore in the Northeast. Number two-eighty. Would you stake yourself out there and grab him if he shows up? Tell him to call me right away at my hotel?"

Myers hesitated. "I was just going to take the girls to a movie. It'd be a shame to disappoint them."

"Sure, I know," Carmody said, rubbing his forehead. "But how about this? Make it tomorrow night and I'll get all three of you tickets to the new musical. And dinner at the Park Club first. My treat."

"A night on the town, eh? Sounds pretty fancy," Myers said dryly.

"Well?"

"By the way, I got an envelope from Degget. Thanks."

"Degget?"

"Yeah, the little character we had in that Wagner Hotel murder. He sent me fifty bucks. And a note. Did you read the note?"

"No," Carmody said impatiently.

"Well, he said the smart detective told him I could use the fifty bucks." Myers laughed shortly. "That's you he meant. The smart detective."

"What're you getting at?"

"Yeah, you're the smart detective," Myers said, the words tumbling angrily from him. "And your brother's in trouble with Ackerman's bums and you want me to help you pull him out. Why don't you go to the hoodlums? They're your buddies, aren't they?"

"Forget it," Carmody said slowly. "I didn't know you felt this way."

"You wouldn't know how I feel," Myers said. "That would mean noticing me, asking me. But you're too much a big shot for that. What the hell was that address?"

"I said forget it."

"Give me that address. I'll get it from the book if you don't. I'm doing this for your brother. Because he's a cop, a dumb honest slob like me. Not for you, Mike."

"It's two-eighty." Carmody wet his lips. "Thanks, Myers."

"Go to hell."

The phone clicked. Carmody got to his feet, rubbing his forehead. What the devil had got into Myers? Had he been keeping this bottled up all these years? And what about the other men on his shift, and in the department? Did they feel the same way?

So what if they do, he thought, frowning and disturbed. It's there to take. If they had the brains they'd take it, too.

There was nothing to do but wait. He tried all the bars, and Eddie's home and district half-an-hour later but drew blanks. He left messages for Eddie everywhere to call him but that was all he could do.

The night deepened beyond his windows, moving slowly in wide black columns to the pink-gray streaks on the horizon. Lights came on in the tall buildings in the business district and the city spread out before him, a powerful exciting mass, cut through and through with white lines of traffic. Eddie was out there somewhere. Standing on a dark corner lighting a cigarette, swinging down a black alley on a short-cut to the district, stopping before a movie to look at the posters. And somewhere out there Ackerman's killer might be starting slowly and carefully to work, asking questions, making calls, closing in on his brother's trail. And all I can do is wait, Carmody thought.

When the phone rang the sound of it went through him like an electric shock. He crossed the room in three strides and jerked the receiver to his ear. "Yes? Hello?"

"Hello, slugger," Beaumonte said with a laugh. "You pack quite a punch, or didn't anyone ever tell you?"

Carmody was caught off balance by Beaumonte's obvious good-humor. "Is that what you called to tell me?"

"No, this is business, Mike. I don't like being knocked

around but I'm going to forget it. There's more at stake just now than a row between friends."

"Tell me about it," Carmody said.

"Ackerman and I had a talk after you left. He wants you to keep working on your brother. You said you could make him listen to reason. Does that still go?"

"Sure I can," Carmody said. The tension dissolved in him and he let out his breath slowly. With time he could work something out. "I'll need a few days," he said.

"Two days is the limit. That's Ackerman's final word."

"Okay, two days then," Carmody said. He was trembling with relief; Eddie wouldn't die tonight. "I can handle it in two days, I think."

"Good. And if you want to pound somebody, well, pound some sense into your brother."

"I'm sorry about tonight, Dan," Carmody said slowly.

"Don't worry about that. Let me know when you've made progress."

"Okay, Dan."

Carmody put the phone down and saw that his hands were trembling. Relief did that to you, just like fear. Eddie was safe for two days. Would it narrow down to hours? And then minutes?

Carmody turned on the record player and walked deliberately to the liquor cabinet. He took out a fresh bottle and put it on the table beside his chair. What had he told Nancy? That he didn't drink because he didn't want to be anyone else. Did that still hold? He sat down slowly, heavily; and let his big hands fall limply on either side of the chair. Not any more. I'd love to be someone else right now, he thought.

Carmody reached for the bottle the way a desperate man would turn on the gas . . .

He was awakened by a sound that seemed to be pounding at the inside of his head. Pushing himself to a sitting position, he stared blankly around the dark room. He checked his watch; the illuminated hands stood at one-forty-five. He had been out for hours. His coat lay beside him on the floor and his collar was open. There was a dull pain stretching across his forehead, and his stomach was cold and hollow.

The knocking sounded again, more insistently this time. Carmody snapped on a lamp, pushed the hair back from his forehead and went to the door.

Nancy stood in the corridor, swaying slightly; the night elevator man held her arms to keep her from falling. "She insisted I bring her up, Mr. Carmody," the man said. "I rang you but didn't get no answer."

"It's alright," Carmody said. "Come in, Nancy. What's the matter?"

She swayed toward him and he caught her shoulders. "Take it easy," he said.

"Beaumonte kicked me out," she said, grinning brightly at him; the smile was all wrong, it was as meaningless as an idiot's. "Got a drink for a cast-off basket case?"

"We can find one." Carmody led her to the sofa, put a pillow behind her head and stretched out her legs. Turning on the lights, he made a drink and pulled a footstool over beside the couch.

"Take this," he said. She looked ghastly in the overhead light; her face was like a crushed flower, lipstick smeared, make-up streaked with tears. "What happened?"

"He kicked me out, Mike. He gave me to some friends of his first. People he owed a favor to. Or maybe I'm flattering myself. Maybe they're people he doesn't like. They took me to a private house near Shoreline." She shook her head quickly. "They were real gents, Mike. They gave me cab fare home."

Carmody squeezed her hand tightly. "Take the drink," he said.

"I don't know why I came here. I shouldn't have. I guess it was seeing you in the fight. You're the only thing they're afraid of."

"Did you hear any talk about me after I left? From Ackerman, I mean? About me or my brother?"

She stared at him, her mouth opening, and then she shook her head from side to side. "Oh God, oh God," she whispered. "You don't know?"

"What?" Carmody said, as the shock that anticipates fear went through him coldly.

Clinging to his hands, she began to weep hysterically. "It's all over town. I heard it from Fanzo's men, and on the radio in the cab. Your brother was shot and killed a couple of hours ago."

7

SHE WAS CRYING so hard that it took Carmody several minutes to get any details. When he learned where it had happened he stood up, his breathing loud and harsh in the silence. "You stay here," he said in a soft, thick voice. He picked up his coat and left the room.

The shooting had occurred a block from Karen's hotel. Carmody got there in twenty minutes by pushing his car at seventy through the quiet streets. The scene was one he knew by heart; squad cars with red beacon lights swinging in the darkness, groups of excited people on the sidewalks whispering to each other and women and children peering out from lighted windows on either side of the street. He parked and walked toward the place his brother had died, a cold frozen expression on his face. A cop in the police line recognized him and stepped quickly out of his way, giving him a small jerky salute.

Lieutenant Wilson was standing in a group of lab men and detectives from Klipperman's shift. One of them saw Carmody coming and tapped his arm. Wilson turned, his tough, belligerent features shadowed by the flashing red lights. He said quietly, "We've been trying to get you for a couple of hours, Mike. I'm sorry about this, sorry as hell."

Carmody stopped and nodded slowly. "Where's Eddie?" he said.

"They've taken him away."

"He's dead then," Carmody said. Nothing showed on his face. "I was hoping I'd got a bum tip. What happened?"

"He was shot twice in the back. Right here."

Carmody stared at the sidewalk beyond the group of detectives and saw bloodstains shining blackly in the uncertain light. In the back, he thought.

"We'll break this one fast, don't worry," Wilson said. "We've got a witness who saw the shooting. She was a friend of Eddie's. Karen Stephanson. You know her?"

"She saw it, heh? Where is she now?"

"At Headquarters, looking at pictures."

Carmody turned and walked away, his heels making a sharp, ringing sound. Wilson called after him but Carmody kept going, shouldering people aside as he headed for his car.

It took him twenty minutes to get back to center-city. He parked at Oak and Sixteenth, a few doors from the morgue, and walked into the rubber-tiled foyer. The elderly cop on duty got to his feet, a solemn, awkward expression on his face. "He's down the hall. In B," he said. "You know the way, I guess, Sarge."

Carmody pushed through swinging doors and turned into the second room off the wide, brick-walled corridor. Three men were present, a pathologist from Memorial Hospital, a uniformed cop and an attendant in blue denim overalls. The square clean room was powerfully illuminated by overhead lights and water trickled in a trough around the edge of the concrete floor. The air smelled suspiciously clean, as if soap and brushes had been used with tireless efficiency to smother something else in the room.

Eddie lay on a metal table with a sheet covering the lower half of his body. The brilliant white light struck his bare chest and glinted sharply on the smears and streaks of blood. His shirt, which had been cut away from him, lay beside the table on the floor.

Carmody stared at his brother's body for a few moments, his features cold and expressionless. A lock of hair was curled down on Eddie's ivory-pale forehead and his face was white and empty and still. The choirboy who stole the show at St. Pat's, Carmody thought. Who wanted to play it straight, get married and have kids. That was all over, as dead as any other dream. One of the men said something to him hesitantly and awkwardly. "Damn shame, sorry . . ." Carmody couldn't speak; a pain was pressing against his throat like a knife blade. He nodded slowly, avoiding their eyes.

Someone came into the room behind him, and Carmody turned and saw old Father Ahearn standing in the doorway.

"I came as quickly as I could, Mike," he said.

Carmody turned and looked down at his brother. "We were all too late," he said, holding his voice even and cold. "Too late, Father." He put out a big hand and pushed the lock of hair back from Eddie's forehead. For another moment he stood there, staring at the pale quiet face, and then, moving deliberately and powerfully, he walked past the priest and out to the sidewalk. The night was cool and soft; a faint wind moved over the city and a diffused light was spreading thinly along the horizon.

The door behind him opened and Father Ahearn came to his side. "Why can't you face me, Mike?" he cried softly. "Who did this thing to your brother?"

"I warned him," Carmody said, swallowing hard against the pain in his throat. "I warned him, but he wouldn't listen to me."

"You warned him!" Father Ahearn took Carmody's big hard arm and tried to pull him around; but the detective's body was like a post set in stone. "What do you mean by that, Mike?"

"He wouldn't listen to me," Carmody said again. "They meant business but he wouldn't believe it."

"You knew this was going to happen?" the old priest said in a soft, horrified voice. "Is that what you are saying?"

"Sure, I knew it would happen . . ." Carmody said.

The old priest took a step backward, quickly and involuntarily, as if the face of evil had appeared before him without warning. "God have mercy on your soul," he said, breathing the words softly.

"Save the mercy for the men who killed him, Father." Without looking at the old priest, Carmody turned quickly and strode toward his car.

Half an hour later he pulled up before Karen's hotel. The street was quiet now, the squad cars had gone back to their regular duty. Only a few groups of people remained on the sidewalk, smoking a last cigarette and exchanging their final words on the shooting. Everyone prefaced his recapitulation with an "I was just—" "Just getting into bed." "Just locking up." "Just opening the ice-box—when it happened." For some reason, Carmody thought, listening to the eddies of talk in the silent street, they all felt these commonplace activities had assumed a shape and significance through their temporal relationship to tragedy. And maybe they did. I was just getting drunk, he remembered. Just passing out after accepting Beaumonte's word that Eddie would be spared for two more days.

A middle-aged patrolman was posted in the small foyer of Karen's hotel.

"Is the witness back yet?" Carmody asked him.

"Got in about fifteen minutes ago, Sarge."

"You'll be here all night?"

"That's right. And there's a man in back and one just outside her room. You going up?"

"Yes." The cop unlocked the inner door and Carmody walked by him and took the elevator up to her floor. He nodded to the alert-looking young cop who was on guard there and then rapped on her door.

"You'd better start asking everybody for identification," he said.

The young man flushed slightly. "I've seen your pictures in the paper lots of times, Sarge."

"Okay. But be on your toes when anyone gets off that elevator. If the guy she spotted comes up here he won't give you a chance. Remember that."

"I'm ready for him," the cop said, putting a hand on the butt of his revolver.

Carmody glanced at his youthful, clean-cut face, and swallowed hard against a sudden constriction in his throat. Another Eddie, confident and hard, willing to take on all the trouble in the city. How did they get guys like this for sixty bucks a week? Where did they find these brave dumb kids?

The door opened and Karen looked up at him. She had been crying but her face was now pale and composed. For a moment they stared at each other in silence. Then she said, "What do you want here?"

"The whole story, everything," he said, moving into the room and closing the door. She sat down slowly and locked her hands together in her lap. "Eddie was killed, that's what happened," she said, struggling to control her voice. "Just the way you said it would."

"You saw the killer. I want to know what he looked like. I want every detail you can remember."

"I've told the police everything."

"Tell me now."

"Why should I? You're a friend of the men who killed him. You stood by and let them murder him." She rose suddenly and turned away from him, her small face beginning to break and crumble with emotion. "You said we were the same kind of dirt, didn't you? But you let them kill your brother. I'm not in that class."

Carmody took her frail shoulders in his hands, twisted her around and sat her in the chair. When she attempted to get up, weeping helplessly now, he caught her wrist and forced her back with a turn of his hand. "I don't want any speeches," he said coldly. "There'll be plenty of speeches from everybody else. The Mayor, the newspapers, priests and ministers, they'll all make speeches. But they won't do any good. When they're all through talking, Eddie will be just as dead. So don't waste my time with a speech." His voice went low and hard, "Start with the beginning. Eddie was here tonight, wasn't he? When I called?"

"Give me just a minute," she whispered.

"Okay, take your time," Carmody said, releasing her wrist. He lit a cigarette and drew the smoke deeply into his lungs. Then he sat down and stared at a picture on the wall. Finally, he glanced at her. "Okay?"

"Yes. Eddie was here when you called. But he told me he didn't want to speak to you. He listened to the conversation and broke the connection when you began to yell at me. I begged him to be careful but he said you were more frightened of Ackerman than he was." She stopped, breathing slowly, and put the palm of her hand against her forehead.

"We watched television until eleven-thirty. When he left I tidied up the room and found his wallet in the chair he'd been sitting in. His badge was clipped inside it and I knew he'd need that on duty. So I went downstairs to see if I could catch him. The street was dark but I saw him walking toward the corner, about fifty yards away. I ran after him. I didn't call because it was late. Eddie didn't hear me until I was eight or ten feet from him. I'd changed into slippers and I didn't make any noise, I suppose. Then he turned around quickly and reached for his gun. When he saw me he laughed and started to say something. But he didn't get the words out." She shuddered and rubbed her arms with her hands. "That's when it happened. A man stepped from behind a tree and into the light of the street lamp. He had a gun and he shot Eddie twice in the back. Then he ran to the corner. I began to scream and he looked around and stopped. He started toward me but a woman came out on the balcony across the street and began to shout for the police. The man stopped again, under the light at the corner, and then he turned and ran into the next block."

"Okay. You've been looking at pictures at Headquarters. Did you find this man in any of them?"

She shook her head slowly.

"Tell me what he looked like. Everything you can remember."

"He was big. Not fat, but tall and wide. His hair was blond and long. I couldn't see his eyes, they just looked black, but his face was heavy and brutal."

"How old?"

"Young, not more than thirty."

"How about his clothes?"

"He was wearing a sports jacket and a sports shirt. The shirt was open at his neck and the jacket was a light color. Gray tweed or camel's hair, something like that."

Carmody frowned. He knew the local hoodlums who might have done this night's work: Sheen in West, Morgan or Schmidt in Northeast, Youngdahl who ran a bowling alley in Meadowstrip. But Karen's description fitted none of them. That meant an imported killer. And you couldn't get a man like that in ten minutes. It required arrangements, discussions, planning. So the double-cross hadn't been a spur-of-the-moment decision. It had been in the works all the time.

He began to smile slowly. "I'll get that man, Karen. Don't worry about it."

"What good will that do? Eddie's dead. You can't bring him back."

"I'm not doing this for Eddie," he said, still smiling coldly. "This is for me. They promised me time to work on him, and I believed them. They lied to get me out of the way. And it worked. Then they shot him down like a dog. Do you think I'll let them get away with that?"

"I might have guessed this," she said, staring at him with something like wonder in her eyes. "It's not for Eddie. It's not because the men who killed him are savage and cruel and evil. It's because your pride is hurt. Their great crime was to make a fool of Mike Carmody. Even your own brother's death can't penetrate your thick-headed arrogance."

"I told you to skip the sermons," he said, getting to his feet.

"I know you don't want to hear sermons," she said bitterly. "You don't want to hear a word about right and wrong or good and evil. Those things hurt you. You can't stand them, Mike."

"Shut up!" he said thickly. "Damn it, will you shut up?"

"No, you don't want anyone to tell you what kind of a man you are. You sneer and laugh at the whole world but you're too damn sensitive to listen to its judgment on you. Well, some day you'll have to listen, Mike. You helped fire the bullet that killed Eddie, and you'll never be able to run away from that fact."

"I did what I could," Carmody said, catching her thin shoulders in his big powerful hands and lifting her to her feet. "Don't ever say I killed him. Don't ever say that to me again."

"You did nothing but advise him to become a thief like you," she said, staring into the pain and fury in his eyes. "When that didn't work you walked away from him. That's what you did, Mike."

The words framed the dark thoughts which he had been fighting to drive into the safe hidden depths of his mind. I didn't kill him, I didn't kill him, he thought, hurling the words like weapons at his growing sense of guilt. Then he released her arms so abruptly that she staggered to keep her balance. "You don't know anything about it," he said hoarsely.

"You're feeling it now," she said, watching his face. "It's something you'll never get away from. If I've done that, I'm glad."

"I'm tougher than you think," he said, forcing a smile onto his lips. "Listen to me; Eddie didn't die because of me. Eddie died because he was a fool."

She sat down slowly, watching him with a frown, and then shook her head sadly. "If you can say that, you're tough all right. You're not a man, you're just a slab of concrete. But some day you'll crack up anyway. And the crash will be that much louder."

"Don't bet on it," he said.

It was four in the morning when Carmody entered his own living room. The lights were on and Nancy Drake lay on the sofa, an empty whiskey bottle within inches of her trailing hand. Strands of her fine blonde hair fell across her damp cheek and there was a little smile on her lips. But it was a stiff, unnatural smile, the kind Carmody had seen on the lips of women who needed to scream. The line of her body was rigid and the smooth muscles in the backs of her calves were drawn up into small knots.

He shook her gently. "How do you feel, Nancy?"

"Feel?" The grin grew wider. "Hotsy-totsy." A spasm shook her body and she pounded her feet up and down on the cushions of the sofa. "Say something nice to me, Mike. Don't let me start crying."

"Let's have a drink. That's something nice, isn't it?"

"Real peachy," she said. "Let's just do that, Mike."

The phone rang suddenly, shrill and ominous in the silence. Nancy cried out softly and Carmody patted her shoulder. "Keep quiet while I'm talking," he said. "Okay?"

"Sure, Mike."

Carmody crossed the room and picked up the phone. "Hello."

"Mike, this is Bill Ackerman."

Carmody stared at the receiver. Then he said softly, "You made a mistake tonight, Bill. I'm going to prove it to you."

"Now get this!" Ackerman's voice was sharp and controlled. "We didn't kill your brother. I promised you forty-eight hours and I meant it. Whoever shot him was working on his own. We'll find the killer and when we do he's all yours. Do you understand me, Mike?"

Carmody smiled coldly. Was this the opening lead in another double-cross? Was he next on the list? "I thought you'd killed him, Bill. I thought you'd crossed me," he said.

"I don't work that way. I don't need to. I gave you forty-eight hours and I stuck to my word. My guess is that some hophead learned that your brother was causing us trouble, and decided to get in good with us by doing the job on him. He'll be in for a handout one of these days and you can take over from here. Is that clear?"

"That's your guess, eh?"

"I can't think of anything else."

The unpleasant little smile was still on Carmody's lips. Ackerman's confidence was almost funny, he thought. But where was this leading? Ackerman hadn't called to explain himself or apologize. There was no reason for that.

"I'm glad you weren't involved in it," Carmody said. "I'm going after the guy who did the job."

"We'll help you, Mike. Is there anything you need right now?"

"I'm okay. I don't need help."

"If you need it, it's here. Now here's why I called. Did you see Nancy Drake last night or this morning?"

Carmody frowned. What was Ackerman's interest in Nancy? "No, I haven't," he said, glancing at the slim figure on the sofa.

"That's funny. She was out with some of Beaumonte's friends last night. The last thing she told them was that she was going to your place."

"My place? She must have been drunker than usual."

"I imagine so. Anyway, Beaumonte wants to find her."

Now it's Beaumonte, Carmody thought. Why should Ackerman give a damn about Beaumonte's troubles? There had to be an answer to that one. Ackerman operated solely in the light of self-interest; nothing mattered to him unless it directly concerned his safety and money. "Did Beaumonte and Nancy have a row?" he asked casually.

"Yeah. He didn't like that baptismal job she did on him."

"Well, I'll check the elevator men here at the hotel," Carmody said. "You want me to go any farther?"

"Sure. Find her if she's still in town."

"Okay." Carmody hesitated, then: "I'll give Beaumonte a call if I get a line on her."

"No, let me know first," Ackerman said. Normally he never explained or discussed his orders, but now he said, "I'll hand her over to Dan as a little surprise."

"Sure."

"And, Mike, I'm sorry about your brother."

Carmody couldn't say thanks to that, the words would have stuck in his throat. "It was a rough deal," he said slowly.

When he put the phone down he walked over and sat down beside Nancy on the sofa. There was a pale morning light coming in the windows now and it glinted on her tumbled blonde hair and the backs of her slim silken legs.

"Can you talk to me a minute?" he asked her quietly.

She twisted around until she was lying on her back. "I'll get out," she said. "I shouldn't have bothered you."

"Don't worry about that," he said, taking one of her hands and rubbing it slowly.

"Why did Beaumonte do it to me?" she asked him in a small, weary voice. Then her eyes began to fill with tears. "I was as good to him as I knew how. I tried my best to do everything he wanted. Really, I did. And he must have liked me a little, Mike. In all the time he never had another girl. He used to laugh about that. Said he was growing old. But that wasn't it. He must have liked me. But he must have hated me, too. That's what I can't understand. Unless he hated me he wouldn't have done this, would he, Mike?"

"He doesn't hate you. He wants you back."

"I don't want to go back," she said, and her hand tightened in his like a frightened child's. "Can he make me?"

"No, of course not."

She sighed. "This is my chance, Mike. I don't want to wind up in some alcoholic ward. I'll lay off the booze, and try to get back into show business. I can do that, I know it."

"That was Ackerman who just called," Carmody said. "He wants you back, too. Does that make any sense to you?"

She shivered and rubbed her bare arms. "It just scares me."

"Is there any reason for him to be afraid of you? Have you got anything on him?"

She shook her head quickly, her eyes bright with fear. "I haven't got anything on anybody, Mike. Tell them that, please, Mike. Even if I could, I wouldn't bother them."

"I'm after them," he said gently. "Because they killed my brother. If you help me they'll never find out about it."

"I was sorry about your brother," she said, beginning to cry. "That was terrible, Mike." She was slipping away from him, he saw, retreating into irrational, nonspecific grief. "They shouldn't have done that."

"You're sure they did it?" He tightened his grip on her hand. "You know they did it?"

"They talked about it after your fight with Johnny Stark. After you'd gone." She stared pitifully at him, transfixed by his cold eyes. "Dan said there was a man tailing your brother, and Ackerman said to tell him to get to work."

Was this what Ackerman was worried about? Carmody wondered. Possibly. But there had to be something else. What Nancy had overheard wasn't evidence. And Ackerman would know that.

"They'll be looking for you," he said. "You told someone you were coming here."

"Don't make me go," she whispered.

"This isn't safe," he said. "Let me think." He had to hide her somewhere. Hotels and boardinghouses were out. If Ackerman were serious he could put a hundred men on her trail. Finally, Karen occurred to him; she was guarded by a detail of police and Nancy would be safe in her apartment. "Come on, let's go," he said. "Fix your hair and get into your coat."

"All right," she said. She seemed to have lost the power

to act or think independently; she moved like a small battered puppet at the touch of his voice.

There was the problem of getting her past the police guard and Carmody put his mind to it on the trip across the dark city. Karen was an important witness, the only lead to Eddie's killer, and the police wouldn't stand for any casual boarders in her apartment. When he parked the car, a half-block from the Empire, he said to Nancy, "Now listen closely. We're going to the Empire Hotel. You can see the entrance from here. You go into the foyer alone and tell the cop that you live in the hotel but don't have your key. That's all, understand? I'll be right behind you and take it from there. Okay?"

Carmody walked into the foyer ten seconds after her and listened as she told her story to the patrolman. Then he said, "It's okay, officer. I've seen her around before. She lives here."

It worked smoothly, not because the cop was careless but because Carmody's endorsement had the stamp of rank and authority on it. In the elevator he punched a button that took them to the floor above Karen's. He led her along the warm silent corridor to the stairway and down one flight to the landing. "Wait right here," he whispered. Then he opened the door and stepped out into the hallway. The young cop stationed at Karen's apartment straightened alertly, but smiled as he recognized him.

"Everything quiet?" Carmody asked him.

"No one's been here since you left."

"Good. I'm going to be here half an hour going

through some pictures with her. Why don't you go down and get some coffee?"

"Well, I'm supposed to stick right here."

"I'll take over. And coffee will keep you sharp the rest of the night."

It was that argument that sold the young cop. "I'll make it on the double," he said.

When the elevator doors closed on him Carmody went down the corridor to the stairway landing and brought Nancy back to Karen's apartment. He rapped sharply on the door and checked his watch. Five o'clock. He wanted to settle this and get to work.

There would be a restless ferment in the city today, precipitated by Eddie's death, and by fear of the cop's reactions to this defiant challenge from the big boys. This was the time to strike, Carmody knew, when people were ready to flinch.

The latch clicked and Karen opened the door. She wore a robe and slippers but he saw that she hadn't been asleep.

"I've got to ask you a favor," Carmody said.

"All right," she said, looking at Nancy.

"She's in trouble with the same guys who killed Eddie," he said. "She needs a safe place to stay."

Karen hesitated, still watching Nancy. Then she put a hand on her arm, and said, "Come on in. There's plenty of room."

"That's mighty hospitable of you," Nancy said, with a pitiful attempt at humor.

"She's had a rough time and is pretty loaded right now," Carmody said. "The cops won't let her stay if they find out she's here, so do your talking with the radio on. And if any detectives come up, put her in the bathroom or kitchen."

"I can manage it," Karen said.

The elevator cables hummed warningly and Carmody closed the door. He was standing with his back to it when the young cop came out of the elevator, carrying two cardboard containers of coffee.

"I brought one for you," he said.

"Fine," Carmody sipped the black coffee slowly, his thoughts ranging restlessly toward the city. The cop was silent until Carmody was ready to leave, then he wet his lips and told him awkwardly and hesitantly how sorry he was about his brother being killed.

"I worked with him and he was all cop," he said.

"I think you're right," Carmody said soberly. Then he left.

8

CARMODY WALKED through the double doors leading to Headquarters at five-thirty that morning. Abrams and Dirksen were there, along with a couple of men from Klipperman's shift. It was their day-off but they had come in when they'd heard the news. The same thing would happen in every station and district in the city, Carmody knew. Off-duty detectives and patrolmen would check in with their sergeants, grimly eager to join the hunt for a cop's killer.

The men stood when Carmody walked in and Abrams made an awkward little speech. "Rotten shame . . . we'll get the son, don't worry . . ." He was clumsy about it because the situation was marred by a make-believe quality; everyone in the room knew who had ordered Eddie Carmody's execution. And why. And they knew Carmody's relationship with Ackerman. But their sympathy was genuine, untouched by these considerations.

"Thanks," Carmody said, his hard face revealing nothing of what he was feeling.

Myers came out of the card room, a solemn expression about his small cautious mouth. "I'm sorry about it, Mike," he said simply. "I staked out at his home last night like you asked me to. But he never showed."

Carmody saw that the detectives were taking in every

word. Well, so what? he thought. Should I be ashamed because I tried to save Eddie's life?

"Thanks, Myers," he said, "you did all you could." Then he turned into Lieutenant Wilson's office. Wilson was sitting at his desk with two empty containers of coffee at his elbow. His square pugnacious face was irritable from lack of sleep. He stood and patted Carmody on the shoulder. For a moment the two men looked at each other in silence, and then Wilson turned away and sat on the edge of his desk. The bright overhead light slanted through the smoky air and drew shadows along the lines of fatigue in his face. "Well, they killed a good boy, Mike," he said at last. "Just like they'd step on a bug."

"You made a proposition to me yesterday," Carmody said. "I'm taking it."

"Turning over a new leaf, eh?"

"I don't know. I can't make any pious speech. I'm a grown man, and I know the world isn't run the way some nun told me it was. But I'm going to get the guys that killed Eddie. That's what counts, isn't it?"

Wilson was silent, studying Carmody with a little frown. "You didn't hear the news, I guess?"

"What news?"

"We've got a new Superintendent of Police. They moved Captain Myerdahl up. Every paper in town is raising hell about your brother's murder. So the Mayor couldn't put a hack for the top job. Myerdahl's first order came in an hour ago. It was one sentence to every captain and lieutenant in the department: get rid of your rotten apples."

That was pure Myerdahl, Carmody thought. The old German was notorious for his shrewdness, his toughness and his defiant, uncompromising honesty. He knew the city as he knew the lines in leathery old hands, and he hated the men who were squeezing the heart out of it for their own profit. Until he retired, or was eased out, Ackerman's gambling operations would be shot to hell. Carmody saw a sharp significance in this; Ackerman must have known what would happen after Eddie's murder. And that meant he was more concerned about taking the heat off Delaney, than he was for the health of his rackets. What Delaney had on him was big!

"You see what that means?" Wilson asked him.

Carmody brought his thoughts back to the point. "I'm your rotten apple, eh?"

"It's a tough time for it to happen," Wilson said, rubbing his tired face. "I know you want to work on your brother's murder. But you're not going to, Mike." He picked up a sheaf of papers from his desk and held them limply in one hand. "This is an unfitness report on you."

"Now wait a minute," Carmody said sharply. "You can't boot me out now."

"If you are going straight for good I might put in a word for you," Wilson said. "But I don't want men who pick and choose their spots to be honest."

"Damn it, are you worried about my soul, or do you want Eddie's killer?" Carmody said.

"I've got an interest in both those deals," Wilson said quietly.

Carmody was silent for a moment or so, staring down at his big hands. "Okay," he said at last. "You aren't stopping me, Jim, you're just making it tougher. I want to work with you, but not at the expense of putting on sackcloth and ashes for Myerdahl's benefit. I'm a crooked cop. Those are dirty words but they fit. They're stuck to me with glue. I can't get rid of them by crossing myself and saying three Hail Marys."

"So you're going to free lance on this case?"

"He was my brother," Carmody said.

"That doesn't give you any exclusive rights. Eddie had five thousand brothers in this city."

"Brother cops, eh?"

"Don't sneer about it, damn you. That's your trouble, Mike. Too much sneering.

"I wasn't sneering," Carmody said impatiently, he got to his feet. "Five thousand or fifty thousand cops won't break this case," he said, staring evenly at Wilson. "If you think so, I'll give you the killer's names as a head start. Ackerman, Beaumonte, Fanzo in Central, Shiller in Meadowstrip. There your murderers are, Jim. Along with assorted goons, bagmen, killers, judges and politicians. They killed Eddie, but you and your five thousand brother cops try to prove it. You won't in a million years. But I will. I know that crowd from the inside and I know the spots to hit." He gave Wilson a short, sardonic salute. "Take it easy, chief," he said, and started for the door.

"Hold on," Wilson said sharply. He got to his feet, his blunt face troubled and undecided. "Working together we can do it, Mike. With the department outside and you inside we could smash them for good."

"Make up your mind," Carmody said. "Am I on the team or off?"

Wilson tossed the unfitness report back on his desk. "I'll hold Myerdahl off somehow," he muttered. Then he looked at Carmody, his eyes sharp and unfriendly. "You get your way always, don't you? Do just what you want and to hell with everybody else."

"Why the analysis?" Carmody asked him. "Let's forget my personality and go to work. What's been going on?"

"We've got a detail of twenty men working out where your brother was shot," Wilson told him. "And when the shops and bars open we're putting out fifty more. Every section is throwing us men. The Vice Squad, Accident Investigation, even the Park guards. They'll fan out from the spot he was killed, making a street by street check of everybody who might have seen the killer. That girl's description will go on the air every fifteen minutes, night and day, to every squad in the city; an eight-state alarm has been out for hours." Wilson rubbed his face. "We'll get him if he's in the city. But that's what I'm worried about. That he may already be gone."

"He's still here," Carmody said. "Don't worry about that."

"How do you know?"

"Listen," Carmody said. The police speaker in the outer room had broken the silence. "To all cars," the announcer said in a flat, unemotional voice. "Be on the alert for murder suspect. Description following. Male, white, age twenty-five to thirty, tall muscular build, blond hair, wide face. Last seen in vicinity of Bering

Street and Wilmer Avenue. Last seen wearing sports jacket, gray or tan, and sports shirt open at collar. This man is armed. Approach with caution."

The speaker clicked twice and was silent.

"That's going out every fifteen minutes," Carmody said. "The killer knows it. Would you move around if you were in his spot?"

"He might have caught a plane twenty minutes after the shooting."

"That might have been the original plan, but I doubt like hell that he followed it," Carmody said. "He flubbed the job. He shot Eddie in front of a witness."

"All the more reason for him to clear out fast."

"Reason for him perhaps, but not for Ackerman. The killer put Ackerman on the spot. And Ackerman won't let him go until it's safe. And it won't be safe until the witness is dead. Or the killer is dead. One or the other. That's why he's still in town. I'll bet on that."

"Then we'll find him," Wilson said sharply.

"Sure you will," Carmody said. "I'm going to work now."

"You've got another lead?"

"I don't know. When I find out I'll check in." Carmody hesitated at the door and looked back at Wilson with a small frown. "Thanks for the break, Jim," he said.

"Never mind that. I wouldn't use you if I didn't have to."

"You're honest at least," Carmody said, smiling crookedly.

He was walking through the bright early morning light

to his car when Myers caught up with him and put a hand on his arm.

"Hold it just a second," he said. "I got something to tell you."

"What is it?" Carmody faced the small detective and tried to keep the impatience out of his voice. The city was coming awake; trolleys jangled on Market Street and the sidewalks were filling up with people. He wanted to be on the move.

"Well, look," Myers said. "Out at the sanitarium where my old lady stays, there's an attendant named Joe Venuti. A long time ago he worked for Capone in Chicago, and he knows the racket crowd pretty well."

"I've heard of him," Carmody said. "He's still wanted on some old charges, I think."

"Yeah, I guess he is," Myers said shrugging. "But he's been going straight for years and he's always been a big help with the old lady. You know how Italians are. They're the best people in the world with sick people and babies."

"What's the rest of it?" Carmody said.

"Sure. That's why I never bothered him I mean. Well, this morning I drove out there and woke him up. I gave him the girl's description of the killer. And he's going to call Las Vegas and Chicago tonight and gossip with some of his old friends."

"How come he's willing to help?"

"He's got to," Myers said, a grim little line going around his mouth. "I put it that way."

Carmody looked at him, slightly surprised. "He might

turn something up, at that. But you watch yourself, Myers. Don't get hurt."

"You don't think I'm much of a cop, do you?" Myers said, smiling slowly at him. "Well, never mind that. Maybe I'm just a little dummy. But I can come up a notch or two for cop killers. I don't like them, Mike."

Brother cops, Carmody thought, studying the little man with a puzzled frown. Sighing he said, "You're okay, Myers. Don't worry about it."

"I'll find you when I hear from Venuti," Myers said, and Carmody saw that his tribute meant nothing to the little detective.

"Do that," he said slightly puzzled and angry. "And thanks."

Forty-five minutes later Carmody walked into the small lobby of the Milford Hotel, a quiet commercial establishment off Market Street. He had stopped at his hotel to shower and change. The loss of a night's sleep hadn't marked him; his eyes were clear and cold, and the muscles of his body were poised like powerful springs.

Showing the clerk his badge, he asked if Johnny Stark was in his room.

"Yes, sir. Shall I ring him?"

"No, I'll go up."

"Yes, sir. Of course."

Carmody rode up in the elevator and rapped twice on Stark's door, shaking the panels with his big knuckles.

Bedsprings creaked after a moment, and Stark said, "Who's that?"

"This is Mike Carmody. Open up."

There was a short silence. Then: "Sure, Mike. Right away."

The door opened and Stark blinked at Carmody, an uneasy smile touching his bruised lips. He wore a bathrobe and his face was thickened and dazed with sleep. "Come in," he said, still smiling uneasily. "I was asleep, out for the count."

"Where did you take Nancy Drake last night?" Carmody asked, walking into the small stuffy room. Stark cocked his good ear at him, frowning with the effort to hear. "Nancy Drake? What about her?"

"Where did you take her?"

Stark rubbed his big hands together, frightened and uncertain. "How'd you know that?"

"If they needed a delivery boy, you'd do. So where did you take her?"

"To Fanzo's bar in Central. I left her there and came home. That's all I did."

"Did you talk to her about anything on the way?"

"No." Stark wet his battered lips and looked away from Carmody's eyes. "She just did a lot of crying."

"What happened when you got there?"

"A guy I never saw before took her away. They were expecting us, I guess. Then I came home."

Carmody turned toward the door but Stark grabbed his arm. "Don't go, Mike. I want to tell you something."

"Take your hand off me."

"All right, all right," Stark said quickly. "But listen to me. Ackerman fired me, Mike."

"That figures, doesn't it?"

"Sure; I'm supposed to be a fighter, not a clown. But

that's not what's worrying me." Stark took a deep breath and rubbed a hand over his lumpy, unintelligent face. "I shouldn't have taken her to Fanzo's. That's what I'm trying to say. She was crying like hell and she begged me not to. It was a lousy thing to do."

"Well, why tell me about it? If you've got troubles go find a bartender or a priest."

"I just wanted to say it," Stark said. "I shouldn't have done it. Can I square it some way? Could I go out to Fanzo's and knock some heads together?"

"Stay away from there. They'd use you for a pin cushion."

"I'm a bum, I guess," Stark said, a little flush of anger coming up under his eyes. "Say it a thousand times. Go ahead. But are you any better? You work for 'em, too, don't you?"

"We aren't in a moral beauty contest," Carmody said, walking out of the room.

Stark followed him to the elevator in his bare feet, twisting his hands together anxiously. The anger was gone from his face; he looked scared and nervous. "One thing, Mike. Just one thing," he said. "You said Ackerman fixed all my fights? Was that straight?"

"No, the fix wasn't in," Carmody said, jabbing the elevator button impatiently. "What difference does it make?"

"It makes a difference to me," Stark said. "Don't you understand that?"

"Okay, I understand," Carmody said. "Go back to sleep."

"You don't believe I'm sorry about taking her out

there, do you?" Stark said. "People can be sorry about things, can't they?"

"Sure they can," Carmody said shortly. "And they always are. But it doesn't do one damn bit of good."

"It makes you feel like less of a heel," Stark said. "It does that much."

Carmody didn't bother answering. The elevator door opened and he stepped in, glad to be leaving Stark and his big soggy burden of guilt.

Fanzo's bar had the name REALE lettered in gilt across a wide plate-glass window. This was his home and headquarters; he lived above the taproom in a large gaudy apartment. Carmody parked his car and locked the doors. Central was that kind of neighborhood. Pool rooms, bars, pizza joints, littered streets, dismal alleys. The city's cesspool. Carmody walked into the tavern and nodded to the bartender, a tall, solemn Negro who wore a white apron pulled tightly across his big stomach. There were a dozen odd men lounging at the bar and in the wooden booths along the wall, bookies, minor hoodlums, all conspicuous and identifiable by their sharp clothes and casually insolent manner. They lived off the honest sweat of fools, and the knowledge of their cleverness had stamped arrogant little sneers on their faces.

"Is Fanzo around?" Carmody asked the bartender.

"Yes, sir, Mr. Carmody. He's upstairs. Want me to tell him you're here?"

"Never mind."

The bartender smiled, his teeth flashing in his solemn face. "You know he don't like being disturbed, Mr. Carmody."

"I'll remember to knock," Carmody said.

He walked through the bar, followed by a dozen pairs of alert eyes, and went up two flights of wooden stairs. The air was close and smelled of heavily spiced foods. Carmody knocked and the door was opened by a slim, dark-haired girl in a red silk robe and pink mules. She was eighteen or twenty, and very beautiful. Her skin was flawlessly smooth, the color of thickly creamed coffee, and her eyes were wide and clear.

"What is it?" she asked him sullenly.

"I want to see Fanzo."

"He expects you?"

From the front of the apartment, Fanzo called out in a high irritable voice: "Who the hell is that? Bring him in here, Marie."

The girl studied Carmody, her lips twisting into a smile. "Go in," she said, moving aside a few inches. Carmody brushed past her and walked through a short hallway to the living room, which was crowded with expensive inappropriate furniture and hung with heavy red draperies.

Fanzo was sitting at a wide table, eating breakfast. When he saw Carmody he got to his feet, a smile replacing the frown on his thin, handsome face. "Well, well, long time no see, keed," he said. "How's the boy? Tough about your brother, hey? I just been reading about it. A cop leads a hell of a life, don't he? No dough, nothing. And always the chance of that big boom sounding behind him." Fanzo shook his head and picked something from a front tooth. "Real tough. You had breakfast?"

"I'm not hungry."

"I'll go ahead. Funny thing, but when I read about people getting killed it makes me hungry as hell. Can't seem to get enough food." He sat down and gestured impatiently at the girl who was leaning in the doorway, one foot crossed over the other, a small smile twisting her full red lips. "Go find something to do," Fanzo said, waving her away with a thin nervous hand. "Go play with the television. Beat it."

She shrugged and sauntered from the room. Fanzo stared after her, smiling at her small round hips and the backs of her bare brown legs. "Screwball," he said, winking at Carmody. He picked up a peach from the bowl of fruit on the table and bit into it strongly, tearing a chunk free with big white teeth. "She's a Mexican. Slipped into Texas under a load of avocados. No entrance papers, nothing. She's crazier than hell. But she's all right. And she does what she is told because if she don't she knows I'll turn her over to the immigration people." Fanzo laughed and picked up his knife and fork and began to eat. There was a staggering assortment of food on the table; eggs, bacon, ham steaks, sausages, enchiladas, cold melon and a variety of breads and rolls. "What's on your mind, Mike?" he said. "You go ahead and talk. I'll eat."

"We're both going to talk," Carmody said.

"Sure, we both talk," Fanzo said, chewing away vigorously. He was a tall lanky man in his early forties, with thin, cold features and glossy black hair. Fanzo's conception of luxury was fundamental and primitive; women, flashy cars, quantity rather than quality in food and liquor. He was a shrewd and powerful factor in the racially mixed jungle that made up Central. Unlike Beaumonte, he had no pretensions about himself; he was a slum-bred hoodlum who lusted for power and cash. Respectability wasn't his goal; he couldn't buy it so he didn't want it. He put no stock in anything that didn't have a price tag on it. But in his district he held more power than Beaumonte did in West. The district made the difference. In Central, crime stalked the gutters and alleys like a bold cat. The city didn't care about murders in this area. They weren't news. And this indifference gave Fanzo a green light. He could enforce his orders by gun or knife, without fear of reprisal. Everyone in Central knew this and so they tried earnestly and fearfully to stay in line.

"What happened to Beaumonte's girl last night?" Carmody said.

Fanzo smiled briefly as he loaded his knife with food. "She's his girl, keed. You better ask him."

"She was brought out here by Johnny Stark. What happened after that?"

Fanzo lowered his knife and looked up at Carmody, still smiling slightly. But his flat brown eyes were irritable. "Mike, I don't like this hard talk," he said. "You come in here like a cop, for God's sake. Put that away, keed."

"Start talking," Carmody said. "I'm in a hurry."

"You know, keed, you're making me mad," Fanzo said, looking at Carmody with a puzzled frown. "I like you, but you're making me mad." He gestured with both hands, a flush of anger staining his thin face. "What's the deal, keed? You break up my breakfast, like you're grilling some punk." He stood up abruptly, throwing his napkin aside furiously. The short leash on his temper had snapped. "Damn you," he said angrily. "Spoil a man's morning food on him. You beat it, Mike. You beat it, you son of—"

Carmody hit him before the word was completed on his tongue. He struck him across the face with the flat of his hand and the impact of the blow knocked Fanzo sprawling over the table. Carmody picked him up from the floor and dropped him into a chair. "Now talk," he said.

There was blood on Fanzo's lips and a smear of egg yolk on the white silk scarf he wore about his neck. He was breathing rapidly, his eyes flaming in his white face. In a high, whinnying voice he began to curse Carmody, spitting out the words as if they were dirt he was trying to get off his tongue.

"That's all," Carmody said softly. "Don't say anything else."

Fanzo paused as a strange fear claimed him completely; looking up at Carmody, he knew that he would die if he said another word.

They were silent for a moment, motionless in the gaudy room. Then Carmody said, "Tell me about the girl. Fast."

"Beaumonte sent her out with the fighter," Fanzo said, watching the detective carefully. "Before that, he called me and told me she needed a lesson. I didn't want to mix into this thing." Fanzo spoke slowly, never taking his eyes from Carmody's face. "Mixing with other guy's broads is no good. He takes her back tomorrow, next week and then he's mad at me for mixing in it. Mad at me because I know he's afraid to take care of her himself. But I do what Beaumonte says. I give her to three, four of the boys and they take her to a place of ours near Shoreline. Nothing real bad happens to her. You know what the boys would do with a little pink-and-white dish like that, they'd just—"

"Never mind the details." Carmody was having trouble controlling his voice. "What happened afterward?"

"They put her in a cab. She said she wanted to go to your hotel. She was kind of wild, still pretty drunk, too, I guess. She did some crazy talking."

"What kind of crazy talking?"

"She said she was going to put Ackerman and Beaumonte in jail." Fanzo smiled cautiously. "That kind of crazy talking."

"Anything else?"

"That's all the boys told me."

"Where are the boys now?"

"I could get them here. But it would take a few hours."

Carmody didn't want to wait that long. Later, if this lever wasn't strong enough, he could come back. Turning he started for the door, but Fanzo said, "Just a minute, Mike."

Carmody looked around. Fanzo was on his feet, holding one hand against the angry red mark on his cheek. "You shouldn't have hit me, Mike," he said slowly. "We were friends, but you put an end to it. I'll come after you some day. Sleep with that from now on, keed."

Friends? Carmody thought. Yes, he had given Fanzo the right to call him friend. They advanced the same interests, took their crumbs from the same table. They were closer than most brothers. Closer than he had been with Eddie. Why had he let this happen? he wondered. Why had he tossed away the privilege of having Fanzo as an enemy?

Walking back across the room, Carmody slipped the revolver from his holster and hefted it in his big hand. "You won't come after me, Fanzo," he said. His voice was soft and the strange cold smile was on his lips. "Because if you do, I'll feed you six inches of this barrel and then I'll put a bullet through your head. So you aren't coming after me, because you're smart, Fanzo."

Fanzo sat down slowly, his eyes dilating as he stared at the cold blue barrel of the revolver. Suddenly he felt cold and weak, as if he had just discovered that this grip on life was tentative and slippery. "No, I won't come after you, keed," he said, and wet his dry lips.

"That's very smart," Carmody said.

He left the room and went quickly down the stairs. A dozen heads turned as he stopped at the door of the smoky bar, a dozen pairs of eyes watched him alertly but cautiously. Everyone knew what had happened; the word had already come downstairs. A crooked cop had gone haywire and slugged Fanzo. But no one moved. The bartender discovered a spot on the bar that needed wiping, and someone whistled aimlessly into the silence. They all knew the legend of this particular cop and none of them was eager to add to its luster. For a moment Carmody let his cold eyes touch every face in the room, and then he walked through the bar and out to the sidewalk.

When the door swung shut a heavily built young man looked anxiously up toward Fanzo's apartment. "We should have stopped him," he said. "Fanzo won't like it that we just let him walk out."

The man beside him grinned. "Why didn't you stop him, boy? You lived a pretty full life, I guess."

9

ACKERMAN REPLACED the phone, checked his watch, and then walked slowly down the sunlit length of Beaumonte's living room. There was an angry glint in his glassy black eyes, but his hard tanned face was expressionless. He glanced at a man who stood at the windows, and said, "Hymie, leave us alone for a few minutes. Go wash your hands or something."

"Sure, boss," Hymie Schmidt said. He was a slender, neatly dressed man with a pale narrow face and thinning brown hair. There was a nervous, charged quality about him, although his body was poised and deliberate in all its movements. The tension was in his dark eyes, which flicked nervously and restlessly from side to side as if constantly on the alert for trouble. "I'll go wash my hands," he said.

"And don't call me boss," Ackerman said shortly. "I'm Mr. Ackerman. Remember that."

"Sure, Mr. Ackerman," Hymie said. His dark eyes flicked angrily from side to side, but avoided Ackerman's. He didn't like this, but he kept his mouth shut. There was no percentage in being mad at Bill Ackerman.

"Come back if you hear the doorbell ring," Ackerman said.

"Right, Mr. Ackerman."

When he had gone Ackerman's mouth tightened

slowly into a flat ugly line. He looked down at Beaumonte, who was slumped on the sofa in a blue silk dressing gown, and said very quietly, "That was Fanzo on the wire. Carmody just left after slapping him around like a two-bit punk. He's looking for Nancy."

Beaumonte rubbed a hand wearily over his forehead. The lack of sleep showed in his face; his eyes were bloodshot and tired, and his flabby cheeks and jowls needed the attentions of his barber and masseur. "I'm sorry," he said heavily. "I'm sorry, Bill."

"That doesn't do one damn bit of good," Ackerman said coldly. "I thought you had more brains than to spout off to a dame. Can't you impress them any other way?"

"I don't ever remember telling her," Beaumonte said, still rubbing his face wearily. "I must have been drunk."

Ackerman swore in disgust. "We've got enough trouble in town without worrying about where she is and who she's talking to," he said.

"We'll find her," Beaumonte said. "We got a dozen guys on her trail."

"And how about Carmody? Anybody watching him?"

Beaumonte nodded. "Sammy Ingersoll. But he hasn't got on him yet. Right now he's downstairs in the lobby. There's a chance Mike will turn up here."

"She's our number one job," Ackerman said. "I know she's been to Carmody's hotel. A cleaning woman remembered her. But the elevator men played dumb. Carmody's trained them not to talk about his business. It's an example you could damn well follow."

A touch of color appeared in Beaumonte's cheeks. He

looked at Ackerman and said, "Let's don't get so mad that we forget business. You think Carmody believed you? About his brother, I mean."

"I don't know," Ackerman said slowly. "He's hard and he's smart. I'll never underestimate him again. That's why I told him to look for Nancy. I figured he'd reason it this way: if Ackerman wants me to find her, he isn't worried about her. So to hell with it." Ackerman shrugged. "I thought he'd think it was just another job and ignore it. But he didn't. He put aside looking for his brother's killer to look for Nancy."

"We'll find her first," Beaumonte said.

"We'd better. Remember that, Dan, we'd better."

Beaumonte got slowly to his feet and smoothed the wrinkled front of his dressing gown. "Just one thing I want clear," he said, meeting Ackerman's eyes directly. "She's not going to be hurt."

Ackerman grinned contemptuously at him. "You threw her out, remember," he said. "You gave her to Fanzo."

"All right, I did it," Beaumonte said, in a thick angry voice. "But I'm getting her back, understand? And in one piece."

"All right," Ackerman said easily. "That's the last thing in the world I want to do, as a matter of fact; you and I are friends, Dan. When we find her I'll send her on a vacation to Paris or Rio or Miami. Anywhere, as long as it is far away and she keeps her mouth shut."

"We understand each other then," Beaumonte said. "She'll be sensible, I'll guarantee that."

Five minutes later the doorbell rang. Beaumonte

started to answer it but Ackerman stopped him with a gesture. "Hold it," he said quietly.

Hymie Schmidt appeared from the study, one hand in the pocket of his coat, his dark excited eyes switching from one side of the room to the other. Ackerman nodded toward the front door and Hymie moved to a position where he could cover anyone who entered. "All right now," Ackerman said to Beaumonte. "Go ahead."

Beaumonte walked across the room and opened the door. Mike Carmody stood in the corridor, his big hands at his sides, a faint cold smile twisting his lips.

"Hello, Dan," he said gently.

Beaumonte took an involuntary step backward. "We were hoping you'd show up," he said, breathing heavily.

"Sure," Carmody said. He walked into the room, and nodded to Ackerman and Hymie Schmidt, whom he knew to be fast and dangerous with a gun.

"You can relax, Hymie," he said, and smiled unpleasantly at him. "We're all friends here."

"I never relax," Hymie said, returning his smile. "The doc says it's bad for my nerves."

Beaumonte moved to Carmody's side, keeping carefully out of the line between the detective and Hymie Schmidt. "I'm sorry as hell about your brother, Mike," he said. "Ackerman told you that it wasn't our job, I know. But I want you to know I'm sorry."

"Sure," Carmody said, nodding. Nothing showed in his face. He had come here because it was essential to convince them that he was back on the team. Only by re-establishing that relationship could he set himself free to rip them apart from the inside. But it would take a hard, careful control to play this out, he realized. More than he had maybe. A dozen hours ago he had stood here fighting for Eddie's life. He had sworn that his brother wouldn't die and Eddie was now laid out in some undertaker's back room. But nothing else had changed; Beaumonte and Ackerman were still healthy and alive, making plans to perpetuate and enjoy their power and rackets. Only the poor grown-up choirboy was gone from the scene.

This went through Carmody's mind as he stared into Beaumonte's anxious eyes. "Well, it's all over," he said. "Talking won't bring the kid back."

"I told you we'll find the killer," Ackerman said. "When we do he's all yours. That's settled." He lit a cigarette and glanced through the smoke at Carmody. "Now, we'll get on to something that isn't settled. I had a call from Fanzo. He tells me you beat hell out of him. What's the story there?"

Carmody smiled slightly. "He called me a name I didn't like. Also, he wasn't being helpful. I traced Nancy to his place, and asked him about her. He got lippy so I had to calm him down."

Beaumonte put a hand on his arm. "What did you find out about her, Mike?"

Carmody turned to him and shrugged. "Nothing at all," he said. He was slightly surprised at the pain in Beaumonte's face. He must have loved her, he thought. The imitation lady, the little bottle girl, Beaumonte's true love. It was almost comical.

"Fanzo had no lead on her?" Beaumonte asked him anxiously.

"He was no help."

"She shouldn't have run off, damn it," Beaumonte said, rubbing his forehead.

"She was at your hotel, Mike," Ackerman said. His eyes were on Beaumonte, warning him to keep quiet.

"Was she?" Carmody said, turning to Ackerman. "I'm sorry I missed her."

Ackerman studied him for a few seconds. "One of the cleaning women saw her. But the elevator boys didn't know anything. Probably she just went through the lobby."

"That's odd," Carmody said, making a mental note to take good care of the elevator boys. Then he shrugged. "What's all the fuss about? She's raddled from too much booze, and scared to death after the job Fanzo's boys did on her. She'll turn up when she's had a night's sleep. Can't you wait a day or so until she comes to her senses?"

"No, we can't," Ackerman said. "Beaumonte wants her back right away because he thinks she's a cute kid. I want her back for another reason. She walked out of here with a bundle of bills, Mike, sixty-two thousand bucks to be exact. I want it back, and fast."

"Now that makes sense," Carmody said. He tried to keep the excitement from showing in his face. When they started lying they were scared. "How'd she get her hands on that kind of money?"

"Dan left the numbers pay-off for Northeast laying around," Ackerman said, shaking his head disgustedly. "So we've got to find her."

"Sure," Carmody said. "I'll let you know if I hear

anything. By the way, Myerdahl's set to clamp down hard. I guess you know that."

"Let me worry about it, Mike," Ackerman said. "This is the seasonal slump in our racket. There'll be raids, arrests, public displays by all the reform groups. Our boys will have it rough for a while. But these things blow over."

"I wouldn't mind a fight," Beaumonte said. "We've made some of the biggest men in this town. If they try to unload us I'd like the chance to ruin the bastards."

"There isn't going to be any fight," Ackerman told him coldly. "I'm not tossing this city up for grabs. Remember that."

Carmody couldn't help marveling at their cool arrogance. The city was their private hunting ground, created and maintained for their express pleasure. They fed on it. Like protected vultures. How did they do it? he wondered. Just how in God's name did they do it? He remembered a phrase of his father's; in weakness there is strength. The old man had used it to spur them on in school. If you were weak at something, but worked like the devil on it, you would become strong through the weakness. Ackerman used a variation of the principle; the city's weakness was his strength. The average citizen's indifference, cynicism and willingness to compromise, was the weakness that Ackerman used as the foundation of his power.

"You'll keep in touch?" Ackerman asked him as he picked up his hat. "Remember, nothing's changed."

"Sure, nothing's changed," Carmody said. Just Eddie, he thought, forcing a small smile to his lips. Yesterday he'd been alive, today he was dead. That was the only change. "I'll keep in touch," he said to Ackerman. "Don't worry."

Downstairs in the lobby Carmody put through a call to Lieutenant Wilson. "I'm just checking," he said, when Wilson answered. "Any progress yet?"

"No. We've got seventy men in the street and they haven't turned up a lead. But I'm glad you called. A guy has phoned here three times wanting to talk to you. He says he's got some information you can use. He wouldn't tell me anything else, except that he was phoning from a drug store and not to bother tracing the call. I gave him your hotel number, and the number of your brother's home. He said he'd try both places till he got you."

"Okay," Carmody said. "He's probably a gravestone salesman. Now look; I suggest you start digging into Ackerman's background immediately. There's a loose end in his past that can trip him up, I think."

"The D.A. has covered that ground before, Mike. Ackerman always kept in the clear. You know that."

"I don't run the department, it's just a suggestion," Carmody said. "But take it to heart, Jim. I know what I'm talking about."

Wilson hesitated. Then he said, "I'll pass that upstairs. You got anything specific in mind?"

"No, that's the trouble. It could be anything, any time."

"I'll pass it on. Keep in touch."

"Of course, Jim," he said.

Half an hour later Carmody parked his car before Eddie's home in the Northeast. It was almost noon then.

Sunlight filtered through the chestnut trees along the block, and faded to a softer tone as it struck the pavements and lawns. The kids playing ball in the street stopped their game to watch Carmody with round solemn eyes. They all know Eddie's dead, I guess, Carmody thought. He was probably a big favorite with them.

The front door was unlocked and he went inside. For a moment he stared about at the familiar furniture and pictures, frowning slightly. Then he walked upstairs to Eddie's room, which was at the rear of the house, overlooking the backyard. He had come here for two reasons: to look through Eddie's things and to wait for a call from the man who had been trying to reach him at Headquarters. Carmody went through Eddie's closet, drawers, desk, looking for nothing and anything. Eddie might have made notes of his identification of Delaney, or he might have noticed that he was being tailed and kept a record of that. Working with trained speed, Carmody opened insurance policies, police department circulars and a bunch of old letters, most of them yellowing notes he had scribbled to Eddie when he was away at school. In the bottom drawer of the bureau were athletic programs, news clippings, class pictures, English compositions with inevitable titles: My First Vacation, When I Grow Up, The Pleasures of Daily Mass. And there were pictures of Mike Carmody, dozens of them; running with a football, getting set to pitch, smiling in his rookie's uniform. There's nothing here, he thought bitterly, unless someone wanted details of the great Mike Carmody's career.

Downstairs again, he stopped with his hands on his hips and looked around the cool dim living room. He frowned at his father's big upright piano, and wondered why Eddie had never got rid of it. It was a space waster and dust trap. But the room played its usual trick on him; the gentle eyes of the *Madonna* stared at him reproachfully; the silent piano and empty chairs made him guiltily aware of the old rupture between him and his father. Exasperated with himself, he picked up a stack of music from the piano and looked at some of the titles. It was the old Irish stuff. *Kevin Barry; Let Erin Remember the Days of Old; O, Blame Not the Bard; Molly Brannigan.* Carmody had heard his father sing them all a hundred times. What had he got out of these songs? Each one told the same poignant story of betrayal and death, of vanished glories, of forsaken people dying grandly in fruitless battles for betrayed causes. Why did he cherish these bitter memories? They belonged a thousand years in the past; why were they important to him in America?

Footsteps sounded on the porch and Carmody put the music back in place hastily. The front door opened and Father Ahearn came into the living room, fanning himself with a limp Panama hat. He stopped in surprise when he saw Carmody standing in the shadows by the piano. "Well, this would make the devil himself believe in miracles," he said. "Coming up the street, I said a little prayer I'd find you here. I wanted to talk to you about Eddie." He sat down slowly and rubbed his eyes with a trembling hand. "The arrangements, you know. I can't get it through my head that the boy is gone."

"About the arrangements, you do what you think is right," Carmody said.

"As a matter of fact, I've done just that," the priest said. "But I thought you'd like to know. The wake will be at Kelly's, starting tonight at eight. Thursday morning at ten there'll be a Requiem High Mass at St. Patrick's. Eddie's district is supplying fifty honorary pallbearers, and the Superintendent is coming. And the Mayor, too, if he can possibly make it."

"That's great," Carmody said.

"It's good of them," Father Ahearn said, nodding slightly, and ignoring Carmody's sarcasm. "Now about the actual pallbearers. I've got five of his good friends from the neighborhood. I've left a place open for you, Mike."

Carmody turned away from him. "You'd better get someone else, Father. I'll be busy."

"Too busy to go to your brother's funeral?" the old priest said softly.

"That's right." He was staring at the music on his father's piano, a bitter look in his eyes. Maybe the old songs had a point. Betrayal and death. They were themes to haunt a man. "I'll be busy looking for his killer, Father," he said. "Let the Superintendent and the Mayor make a show at the funeral. They've got time, I haven't."

"So you're going to avenge Eddie," Father Ahearn said thoughtfully. "In that case, you're a bigger fool than I imagined. You can't avenge him, Mike. Don't you understand that much about yourself?"

"What are you talking about?"

"You don't believe in right and wrong," Father Ahearn said, shaking his head angrily. "In your heart you believe Eddie was killed because he was stupid. Because he wasn't like you. According to the rules you've made, there's no such a thing as sin. So how can you hate something that doesn't exist? By your standards, the men who killed him did no wrong. So how can you hold them to an accounting?" The old priest stood slowly, staring at Carmody with angry, impatient eyes. "Have the guts to be logical at least," he said. "You made the rules to suit yourself, so stick to them, man. Don't think you can flop from one side to the other like some sort of moral acrobat. It won't work, I tell you. You've lost the privilege of hating sin. That belongs to us poor fools who believe in right and wrong."

"All right," Carmody said slowly. "By my rules, I've got to get the men who killed Eddie. Right or wrong, you watch."

"It will do you no good," the priest said.

"I'm not trying to save myself. I'm after a killer."

Father Ahearn looked at him in silence for a few seconds, all the bright anger fading slowly from his face. "Well, I'll be going on," he said.

"Look, wait a minute. Won't you try to understand this?"

"No, I must be going on," he glanced around the room and shook his head slowly. "There was a lot of goodness and decency here, Mike. Stay a bit. Maybe some of it will soak back into you. Good-by, son."

Twenty minutes after the priest had gone the telephone rang. Carmody answered it and a man's voice said, "Is this Mike Carmody, the brother of that cop who got shot?"

Carmody had waited for the call because he knew the value of tipsters; the man with a grudge, the citizen who wanted to assist the law anonymously, even the busybodies—they had helped to break dozens of his cases.

About one in a hundred tips turned out to be helpful. But there was no short cut to find the occasionally reliable informant. The chronic alarmists and crackpots who flooded the police switchboard with calls every day could only be sifted out by patient investigation.

"Yes, this is Mike Carmody," he said. "Who's this?"

"The name wouldn't mean nothing to you. But I'm sorry about your brother."

"So am I," Carmody said. Would Father Ahearn take exception to that? he thought bitterly. Could he at least be sorry? "Well, what's on your mind?"

"Do you remember Longie Tucker?"

"Sure," Carmody said. The man's voice told him nothing; it was high and thin, with a tremor of nerves or fear in it. "What about Longie Tucker?" he asked. Tucker was a local hoodlum who'd drifted out to California six or eight years ago, a big and brutal man with black hair and blunt dark features.

"He's back in town, that's all. I saw him a couple of months ago. And his hair is gray now. The description of your brother's killer said blond hair. But at night under a street light gray hair might look blond."

Carmody nodded slowly. "Where did you see Tucker?"

"In a taproom on Archer Street, right at the corner of Twelfth. I thought of him when I read about your brother."

"I'll run this down," Carmody said. "Thanks."

"I hope it's him, Mr. Carmody."

"What's your interest in this? Paying off an old score?"

"You might say that," the man said in an unsteady voice. "Longie Tucker killed my son. I couldn't prove it, but he did it all right. And my boy never did any harm to anybody. He just got in the way. Well, I won't bother you with it. But I hope he's the man you want."

The phone clicked in Carmody's ear. He frowned at it a moment, then broke the connection and dialed Police. The record room would know where Tucker was hanging out. He wasn't wanted for anything here, as far as Carmody could recall, but some stoolie would have tipped off the police that he was back in town. The clerk at Record answered and Carmody asked for the chief, Sergeant Hogan. After a short wait Hogan came on, and Carmody asked him about Longie Tucker.

"We had a tip when he drifted back to the city," Hogan said. "The detectives in his district watched him for a few weeks, but he seems to be behaving himself. Wouldn't swear he'll keep it up though. He's a stormy one."

"Where is he living?"

"Just a minute . . . here it is . . . 211 Eighteenth

Street. A rotten neighborhood, and just where he belongs. Anything else, Mike?"

"No, that's all."

Hogan hesitated, then said, "Tough about the kid brother, Mike."

"Yes, it was," Carmody said. "But we'll get the guy who did it."

"You're damn right."

Carmody hesitated a moment after replacing the phone, debating whether to run this down himself, or to pass it on to Wilson. It was now one-thirty. He wanted to see Nancy as soon as possible; now he knew she'd been lying when she said she had nothing on Ackerman. But Longie Tucker was an even stronger lure. When he got into his car he headed for 211 Eighteenth Street.

10

IT WAS AN unpainted wooden building set in the middle of a block of municipal decay. Carmody got hold of the owner, a sullen little Spaniard, and asked him about Longie Tucker.

"There is one man on the third floor," the Spaniard said, shrugging carelessly. "I don't care about his name. Maybe you want that one, eh? I got to tell him."

"You go finish your lunch," Carmody said.

"You copper?"

"You just finish lunch, understand, *amigo?*" Carmody said quietly.

"Sure, I don't care," the man said and closed his door.

Carmody went up the stairs quietly. The wallpaper was torn and filthy, and he breathed through his mouth to avoid the greasy, stale smell of the building. Two doors stood open on the third floor, revealing the interiors of small, messy rooms. The third and last door was closed. Carmody eased his gun from the holster and tried the knob. It turned under his hand. He pushed the door inward and stepped into the room, his finger curved and hard against the trigger of his gun.

Longie Tucker lay fully dressed on a sagging bed, one hand trailing on the dusty floor. The room was oppressively hot; the single window was closed and the air was heavy and foul. Tucker breathed slowly and deeply, his body shuddering with the effort. There was an empty whiskey bottle near his hand, and two boxes of pills.

Carmody shook his shoulder until his eyelids fluttered, and then pulled him to a sitting position.

Tucker blinked at him, confused and frightened. "What's the beef?" he muttered.

Carmody's hopes died as he stared at Tucker's drawn face, at the gray skin shot here and there with tiny networks of ruptured blood vessels. The man was half his former size, a sick, decaying husk.

Tucker grinned at him suddenly, disclosing rows of bad teeth. "I get you now, friend. Mike Carmody. Is that right?"

"That's it," Carmody said, putting his gun away.

"I didn't do the job on your brother," Tucker said. "I couldn't do a job on a fly. I ain't left the room in two weeks. I got the bug in my lungs. Ain't that a riot? I go west and get the con."

"Who killed my brother? Do you know?"

"God's truth, I don't. I heard the job was open but I wouldn't have touched it if I could."

"You heard about it? Did they advertise in the papers?"

"Word gets around."

Carmody rubbed the back of his hand across his forehead and turned toward the door.

"Mike, can you spare a buck? I need something to drink."

"No."

"Coppers," Tucker said, making an ugly word of it.

Carmody looked down at him coldly. "Why didn't you save the money you got for shooting people in the back?" Then, disgusted and angry with himself, he took out a roll of bills and threw a twenty on Tucker's bed. "Don't die thinking all coppers are no good," he said.

"Thanks, Mike," Tucker said, grinning weakly as he reached for the money.

Carmody drove across the city to the Empire Hotel and went up past the police detail to Karen's apartment. She opened the door for him and he walked into the cool, dim room. The shades had been drawn against the afternoon sun and Nancy was lying on the studio couch, asleep, an arm thrown over her eyes.

"Must you wake her?" Karen asked him. "She just got to sleep."

"Yes."

"You have to, I suppose," she said dryly.

"Look, I didn't invent this game," Carmody said. Then he felt his temper slipping; the pressure inside him had reached the danger point. Wilson, Father Ahearn and now Karen. They couldn't wait to give him a gratuitous kick in the teeth. "Stop yapping at me," he said abruptly. "If you think I'm a heel write your congressman about it. But lay off me; understand?"

"I understand," she said. "I'm sorry."

The reply confused him; it was simple and straightforward, with no sarcasm running under it. He sat down on the sofa facing the studio couch and lit a cigarette. "I'll give her a few minutes," he said. "How has she been?"

"Not too good. She cried a lot and tried to leave several times. I gave her a few drinks and that seemed to help."

"She had a rough time."

"Yes, she told me about it," Karen said. She sat down beside him on the sofa and shook her head slowly. "What kind of men are they, Mike?"

"Big men, tough men," he said. "With the world in their pockets. They don't believe in anything but the fix. They never heard of Judgment Day."

She didn't answer him. He glanced at her and saw that she was rubbing her forehead with the tips of her fingers. She was wearing a white linen dress and her hair was brushed back above her ears and held with a black ribbon. The faint light in the room ran along her slim legs as she moved one foot in a restless circle. She looked used up; pale and very tired.

"She told me about your break with Ackerman," she said quietly. "And the fight. She thinks you're the greatest guy in the world." Again her voice was simple and straightforward, with no bitterness or sarcasm in it. "That's why I told you I was sorry. You tried to save him. I didn't know that this morning."

"I was a big help," he said bitterly.

"I can't believe he's dead," she said, moving her head slowly from side to side. "Just last night he sat here full of health and hope and big plans. And now he's gone."

"Well, he lived in a straight line," Carmody said, "no detours, no short cuts." He spoke without reflection or deliberation, but the words sounded with a truth he hadn't understood before; it was something to say of a man that the shape and purpose of his life had remained constant against all pressure and temptation.

"It's been a ghastly day," she whispered.

"You ought to get some rest." Without thinking of what he was doing, he put a hand on her back and began to massage the taut muscles of her shoulders and neck. He felt the malleable quality of her body under his fingers, and the small thin points of her shoulder-blades, and he wondered irrelevantly what held her together, what supported all of her poise and strength. There was something inside her that was impervious to attack. She had countered his contempt with a confident anger, as if hating him was a privilege she had earned. Father Ahearn's words struck him suddenly: *Hating sin . . . belongs to us poor fools who believe in right and wrong.* Was that her pitch? That she was on the side of the angels?

"Don't do that," she said suddenly.

"What's the matter?"

"I don't want you to touch me."

Carmody took his hand away from her slowly. "I'm not good enough, is that it?"

"Don't make a big thing out of it," she said wearily. "I just don't want you to touch me, that's all. Not because I think you aren't good enough and not because I don't like it." She looked at him, her face a small white blur in the dim room. "Can't you understand that?"

"Wait until you're asked before you say no," he said, wanting to hurt her as she had hurt him.

"That's a cheap thing to say. It isn't what I meant, Mike, I was just—"

"Cheap?" he said, cutting across her sentence. "That sounds funny coming from you." There had been a delayed reaction to the feel of her body under his hand; now the memory of it crowded sharply and turbulently against his control. "What about Danny Nimo?" he said, his voice rising angrily. "Would you call that just a little cheap around the edges?"

"Oh, damn you, damn you," she said, pounding a fist against her knee. "That's all you've got on your mind. You're infatuated with evil. Goodness bores you. Because the devil is more exciting to you than God. He's your kind of people, a real sharpie. All right, I'll tell you about Danny Nimo."

"I don't want to hear about it."

"Oh, yes you do. It's low and depraved. It's your meat, Mike."

"Stop it," he said sharply.

"I lived with Danny Nimo for a year," she said. "This was six years ago. Then there was the automobile accident. Danny paid the bills and took care of me for two years although I was in a cast most of that time. That was goodness of a sort, although you'd never understand it. During that time I had plenty of time to think about myself and Danny. I tried to understand why I had got mixed up with him. But I couldn't figure it out. Not neatly and simply, anyway. My father was an electrician, my mother was a good-hearted woman and I'd had a fair education. And I had a little talent for music. It didn't add to the way I was living. Maybe it was the fun of being a racketeer's girl. Living high without working for it. Being on the inside. I don't know. But I did know that I'd taken a big step in a direction I didn't want to go. So when I was well enough to walk I told him how I felt and left him. There's the whole story. Did you get a kick out of it?"

The bitterness in her voice confused him. "I'm sorry I spoke out of turn," he said slowly. "Who am I to be judging people?"

"Excuse me," she said and stood quickly. He saw that she was close to tears.

"Wait a minute. Please. Is it that easy to get out? Like you did, I mean?"

"Easy?" She was silent a moment. Then she laughed softly. "Try it, if you think it's easy. Just say, 'Forgive me, I've been wrong.' That's all. But keep a drink close by. The words may choke you a little."

"'Forgive me,'" he said quietly. "Who do I say that to?"

"To whatever you've got left. Maybe yourself."

Carmody shook his head slowly. He couldn't say he'd been wrong and mean it. And how could anybody forgive himself? It was too simple and pat.

Nancy stirred on the couch, and then sat up suddenly, her eyes bright with fear.

"Relax, everything's all right," Karen said gently. "Lie down and finish your sleep."

Nancy recognized Carmody and drew a long, relieved breath. "Old tough Mike," she said, and put her head down on the pillow. She laughed softly. "I guess I had a bad dream."

Carmody sat beside her and took one of her hands.

She looked cool and comfortable under the single white sheet.

"How do you feel?" he asked her. He heard Karen cross behind him and leave the room.

"Pretty good, I guess."

"Ackerman is afraid of you," he said. "What have you got on him, baby?"

She smiled at him but it was a shaky effort. "My mother told me a man could get anything from a woman if he called her baby," she said.

"Don't play around, please," he said. "You told Fanzo's men you were going to send Ackerman to jail. What did you mean by that?"

Her eyes filled with tears. "I'm afraid, Mike. I don't want to get mixed up in it."

"They can't hurt you," he said. "You're safe here."

"You don't know them, Mike."

"I know them," he said. "They're scared and on the run. If you keep them running you'll be safe. But if they beat this trouble you're in a bad spot. Don't you see that?"

Karen returned and sat at the foot of the couch. For a moment Nancy stared at her in silence, her eyes round and frightened in her childish face. "Should I tell him?" she said softly.

"I think so," Karen said. "It would be a big thing to do."

"All right," Nancy said, the words tumbling out rapidly. "Ackerman is afraid of a man named Dobbs. Dobbs lives in New Jersey. That's all I know, Mike, I swear it."

"Dobbs?" The name meant nothing to Carmody. "How did you find this out?"

"Beaumonte told me. When he was drunk one night. You see, something had gone wrong and Ackerman phoned him and raised the devil for fifteen or twenty minutes. When it was all over Dan was in a terrible mood. He drank a full bottle of whiskey, and then started knocking the furniture around and smashing bottles and records all over the place. I never saw him so wild. When I finally got him to bed, he started talking about Dobbs. He didn't know what he was saying, I knew. But he said that Dobbs was the only guy smarter than Ackerman, the only guy Ackerman was afraid of. It meant nothing at all to me. The next day I pretended I'd been drunk too. Beaumonte seemed a little scared. He asked me half-a-dozen times if I remembered what he'd been talking about, but I played dumb. Listening out of turn is just as bad as talking out of turn."

"You must have used Dobbs' name with Fanzo's men," Carmody said.

"I guess I did," Nancy said sadly.

"And it went back to Ackerman." Carmody stood up and turned the name around in his mind. He knew men named Dobbs but none who fitted the role of Ackerman's blackmailer. "Where's the phone?" he asked Karen.

"In the kitchen."

Carmody went into the tiny kitchen, took the phone from the wall and dialed his Headquarters. When the clerk answered, he said, "I'm looking for George Murphy, the reporter. Is he around?"

"Well, he was here half an hour ago. He said he was

going up to the press room, I think. Wait, I'll switch you."

The clerk transferred the call and another voice said, "Press room."

"Is George Murphy around?"

"Hold on. He's talking to his desk on another phone."

"Okay."

Murphy came on a moment later. "Hello?"

"Mike Carmody, George. Are you busy right now?"

"Nothing that won't keep. What's up?"

"I want to talk to you. Can you meet me at the South end of City Hall on Market Street in about fifteen minutes?"

"Sure, Mike. I'll be the man with the press card in his hatband."

Carmody walked into the living room and said to Karen, "I'm going now." His whole manner had changed; the lead was in his hands and his hunter's instincts had driven everything else from his mind.

"Be careful, Mike," Nancy said. Karen watched him in silence.

"I will." He left the apartment and went down to his car.

Murphy was waiting for him at the north entrance of the Hall, his hat pushed back on his big round head, a fresh cigar in his mouth. He looked sleepy and comfortable, as if he'd just finished dinner; but behind those drowsing eyes was a mind like an immense and orderly warehouse. "Hi, Mike," he said, taking the cigar from his mouth.

"Let's walk," Carmody said. "What I've got is very private."

"Okay."

They strolled across the avenue that wound around the Hall, and started down Market Street, walking leisurely through the crowds that were pouring out of shops and office buildings.

Without looking at Murphy, Carmody said, "I've got the start of the biggest story you ever saw. But I need help. When I get the whole thing, it's all yours. How about it?"

"Let's hear the start of it," Murphy said, putting the cigar in his mouth and clasping his hands behind him.

"Ackerman is afraid of a man named Dobbs," Carmody said. "Dobbs lives in New Jersey. That's all I know. I want you to help me find him."

"It doesn't sound right," Murphy said, after walking along a few feet in silence. "Ackerman's not afraid of anybody. He's got rid of anybody who could hurt him, and don't bet against that."

"My tip is straight," Carmody said. "If we can find Dobbs, and spade up what he's got on Ackerman, then you've got a story."

Murphy took the cigar from his mouth and looked at it as they waited for a light. "The story I'll get is your obituary, Mike. You can't buck Ackerman now. Six months from now, maybe. But the city isn't ready yet."

"I'm ready," Carmody said. "To hell with the city."

"You couldn't keep them from killing your brother,"

Murphy said thoughtfully. "What makes you think you can stay healthy?"

"We're different types," Carmody said.

"I guess you are," Murphy said cryptically. Then he shrugged his big soft shoulders. "Let's walk over to the office. Maybe we can find this Dobbs in the library. But I don't see much hope for it."

They spent the next three hours in the *Express* morgue, studying items on those Dobbses whose fame or notoriety had rated interment in this mausoleum of newsprint. There were obits, news and sports stories, announcements of promotions, luncheons, engagements, divorces, weddings. Murphy pawed through the yellowing clips with patient efficiency, occasionally embellishing the stories with scraps from the warehouse of his memory. Finally, he weeded out all but five clippings. "I'll check these," he said. "Each one of these guys knew Ackerman in the old days. And that's where the dirt is, I'll bet. Here we got Micky Dobbs, the fight promoter. And Judge Dobbs who worked for Ackerman before he retired. And Max Dobbs, the bondsman. Tim Dobbs, the fire chief." Murphy grinned crookedly. "He used to condemn joints that didn't cooperate with Ackerman. And last is Murray Payne Dobbs, who was a big trucker before Ackerman ran him out of the state." He made a pile of the clips and then got up from the table and rubbed the top of his head. "You want me to handle this? I can do it through the paper without causing too much talk."

"Okay. Call me when you learn something."

"Where'll you be? At the hotel?"

"No. I'm staying at the old man's."

Murphy glanced at him queerly. "I thought you hated that place."

"It's quieter out there," Carmody said.

At ten-thirty that night a slim, dark-haired man stepped into a telephone booth, fished in the return slot out of habit then dropped a coin and dialed a number. When a voice answered, he said, "Sammy Ingersoll. I got a message for Mr. Ackerman."

"Just a minute."

"What's the word?" Ackerman said, a few seconds later.

"Carmody's bedded down for the night. At his brother's home in the Northeast. He's been huddling most of the evening with a guy from the *Express*. Murphy."

"What about the girl?"

"Only got a guess so far. But it's a good one, I think. She's stashed away in the apartment of that dame who saw the shooting. Karen something-or-other."

"You don't get paid for guessing," Ackerman said angrily.

"I know, Mr. Ackerman. But Carmody took some dame there. I got that from a neighbor who was up early with an earache. This neighbor saw Carmody and the girl go in about four in the morning. I can't check it because they got police guards there. In the lobby and up at her apartment."

"All right," Ackerman said, after a short pause. "We'll handle the police detail. You've earned a vacation. Take a couple of weeks in Miami and send us the bill. And keep what you told me to yourself."

Sammy made a small circle with his lips. His sharp little face was completely blank. "Mr. Beaumonte asked me to let him know if I learned anything."

"I said to keep it to yourself. You'd better not misunderstand me."

"No chance of that. I'm on my way."

When he left the booth, Sammy wiped his damp forehead with a handkerchief. There was no future in getting in the middle between Bill Ackerman and Dan Beaumonte. Miami seemed like a beautiful idea to him, not just for two or three weeks but maybe two or three years.

11

CARMODY SLEPT that night in his old room. In the morning he discovered that someone had taken care of the things he had left here years ago. His suits hung in plastic bags, and his bureau drawers were full of clean linen. Carmody looked at them for a moment, remembering his father's finicky concern over his and Eddie's things. Neatness wasn't his strong point, but he had worked hard at being father and mother to them, repainting their wagons, trimming their hair, getting after them about muddy shoes and dirty fingernails. "Cleanliness is next to Godliness," he had usually intoned while herding them to the bathroom. I suppose he always expected me to come back, Carmody thought.

He had finished a breakfast of orange juice and coffee when the phone rang. It was Murphy.

"Can I pick you up in about twenty minutes?" he said. "We got some work to do."

"What did you find out?"

"Something damned interesting. I'll be out as soon as I can."

Carmody lit a cigarette and walked into the living room. The early sun slanted through the windows, brightening the somber tones of the furniture and pictures. For some reason the room didn't depress him this morning. He thought about it as he smoked and looked at his father's piano. Ever since he had started trying to save Eddie his thoughts had been returning restlessly to the old man. He should have no time for anyone but Ackerman. His thoughts should be on what Murphy had dug up, but instead they swerved irrelevantly into the past. Back to unimportant details. Like his clothes hanging neatly and cleanly in the closet upstairs. And an image of the old man at the piano booming out something for the Offertory. *Redemptor Mundi Deus.* Even now the somehow frightening Latin words could send a shiver down his spine. But why? They were just words, weren't they?

A footstep sounded on the porch and Carmody went quickly to the door. Father Ahearn smiled at him through the screen. "I just thought I'd see if you were home," he said.

Carmody let him in and the old man sat down gratefully.

"It will be hot today." He sighed and looked up at Carmody. "You asked for understanding from me yesterday but I left you. That wasn't the way for a priest to behave. I'm sorry."

"That's okay."

"I wish I could help you. You know, Eddie gave me his will the last time I spoke with him. He wanted you to have this house. Did he tell you that?"

"No, he didn't," Carmody said slowly.

"You don't want it, do you?"

"I haven't thought about it. But I guess not. Why should I?"

"You're a stubborn man," Father Ahearn said. "Just

like your father. If you understood him, you might understand yourself, Mike. He was a proud man, and very set in his ways. But they were pretty good ways." The old priest smiled slowly. "Remember how touchy he was about his singing. And the truth was he didn't have a very good voice."

"But big," Carmody said.

"Oh, it was that, I grant you." Father Ahearn got to his feet with an effort and went to the piano. "Eddie kept all the music, I see." He picked up one of the sheets and smiled at it. *O, Blame Not the Bard.*" His eyes went across the music. "Twas treason to love her, twas death to defend," he murmured, shaking his head. Then he looked sharply at Carmody. "That's something to remember about your father, Mike. He wasn't allowed to love his own country. Like thousands of other Irishmen, that love was a kind of treason. Can't you understand their bitterness when their sons went wrong over here? Instead of being grateful for a country to love and live in, some of the sons seemed bent only on spoiling the place. That hurt men like your father. It makes them angry and unreasonable, which isn't the best tone to use on hot-headed young men. Can't you see that, Mike?"

"Well, it's all over, anyway," Carmody said. "He's dead and I'm still the rotten apple. Talking won't change it."

"How did you get so far away from us?" Father Ahearn said, shaking his head slowly.

"I don't know. It wasn't one decision." Carmody shrugged. "Little by little, I guess."

"Couldn't you try coming back the same way? Little by little, I mean."

"Admit I've been wrong? Ask for forgiveness." Carmody turned away from him and pounded a fist into his palm. "It's no good. If I did that I'd come to a dead-center stop. And I can't stop while my brother lies dead and his murderers are living like kings." Turning back, he stared angrily and hopelessly at the priest. "All I've got is a certain kind of power and drive. I can do things. The way I am, that is. But I'd be nothing if I turned into a confused sinner, begging for forgiveness."

"You'll be nothing until you see that Eddie's murder was wrong," Father Ahearn said sharply. "Not because he was your brother, or a police officer, but because he was a human being whose life belonged to God."

A car door slammed at the curb. Through the windows Carmody saw George Murphy coming up the walk. "I've got to be going, Father," he said, relieved to end this painful and pointless argument.

"Remember this," the old priest said, and put a hand quickly on his arm. "Don't get thinking you're hopeless. St. Francis de Sales said, 'Be patient with everyone, but above all with yourself.' Keep that in mind. All sinners flatter themselves that they are hopeless. But no one is, son."

"Okay, okay," Carmody said shortly; he wanted to be gone, he wanted no more talk about sin and forgiveness. Turning, he left the house and met Murphy on the front porch.

"We've got to take a ride," Murphy said. "You set to go?"

"Yes."

When Father Ahearn came down the steps, Murphy's sedan was moving away from the curb. He watched until it had disappeared at the corner, and then shook his head and started back to the rectory. His expression was weary and troubled.

"Well, what is it?" Carmody asked, as Murphy headed through the bright streets toward the River Drive.

"The Dobbses we found in the clips didn't add up to anything," Murphy said. He looked tired and hot; his day-old beard was a black smudge along his jaws, and his eyes were narrowed against the sunlight. "I worked all night on them and didn't get a lead. But I found another Dobbs, and he could be our man."

"Who's that?"

"This fell into my lap, from an old guy named Sweeney who's been a rewrite man on our paper since the year One. I got talking to him this morning, and he told me about a Billy Dobbs who worked on the *Intelligencer* years back. Not a reporter, but a photographer. The only memorable thing about Dobbs, Sweeney told me, was that he once stumbled accidentally into a bank stick-up. This was in '38. Dobbs was coming in from a routine assignment, driving south on Market Street, when three guys ran out of the old Farmer's Bank with satchels of dough and guns in their hands. They killed two cops right in the street, and a bullet hit the windshield of Dobbs' car. He stopped and scrambled into a gutter to get out of the fire. All he thought about was taking cover instead of taking pictures. He could have been a hero by photographing the gunmen, but he'd probably have been a dead one. That's what he said, at any rate. Two years later Dobbs quit the paper and that's all Sweeney could tell me about him." Murphy glanced at Carmody. "You see where this might be leading?"

"I've got an idea."

"Right now we're going to where Dobbs used to live. A guy in the *Intelligencer's* personnel section gave me his old address. It's in Avondale, in a pretty average neighborhood. Dobbs lived there with his mother and father. But they've all been gone for a long time."

"We'll have to ring a lot of doorbells to find someone who knew them," Carmody said.

"I can't think of any short cut," Murphy said, and rubbed a hand wearily over his face. "I wish there was. I could use some sleep."

They parked in front of the two-story wooden house in which the Dobbs family had lived, and got out of the car. The street was shady and quiet, in a neighborhood that was deteriorating steadily but gradually.

"You want the odd or even addresses?" Murphy said dryly.

"I'll take the other side. Let's go."

It was in the middle of the afternoon and two blocks from the Dobbs home that Carmody got his hands on a lead. She was a pleasant little woman, starched and clean in a blue house dress, and she had known the Dobbses very well. "Funny you should ask," she said, tilting her gray head at Carmody. "I was just thinking of Ed and Martha the other day. Something brought them back to mind, what I just can't remember. But come in, won't you? No sense baking there in the sun."

In the dim old-fashioned parlor, Carmody said, "Do you remember when they moved away?"

"Yes, it was just before the war. The Second World War, I mean. About '40 or '41. Ed quit his job on the cars, and off they went. To California."

"Did you know their son? Billy Dobbs?"

"Indeed I did. He was a quiet, steady youngster, and got himself a fine job on the paper. Took pictures for them. We used to see his name on them sometimes. Fires, accidents, all sorts of things you'd never expect little Billy Dobbs to be mixed up in."

"But he quit his job, didn't he?"

"That's right. Moved off to another paper. It worried his mother, I can tell you, but it turned out pretty well, I guess."

"Do you know what paper he went to?"

"His mother told me but I forgot," the woman said, with a little sigh.

"Anybody around here ever hear from the Dobbses?"

"No, not for years anyway. Old Mr. Johnson, he's dead now, looked them up when he was in California. He was out seeing his son who was in camp there, you see. And the Dobbses had come into good luck. Some relative of theirs in Australia had died, they told Mr. Johnson, and left them a nice little bit of money. They were living in style, he said. Flower garden, nice home, a maid even." She smiled and shook her head. "A far cry from the days when they were on the cars."

"Was their son around?"

She frowned. "Mr. Johnson never said anything about Billy. . ."

Carmody went quickly down the stairs to the sidewalk and looked along the street for Murphy. He saw him in the next block and yelled at him to get his attention. When Murphy turned, Carmody shouted, "Let's go. I've got it. . ."

"Everything fits," Carmody said, as they headed back toward his home. "Dobbs did take pictures of the stickup. He waited two years, probably protected himself from every angle and then parlayed them into a pension plan."

"Nice guy, Dobbs," Murphy said, nodding. "Didn't forget the old folks either. The thing is, I guess, to find Dobbs."

"We won't find him," Carmody said. "Ackerman has sent him on the road by now. Dobbs is on his way to South America or Newfoundland, I'd bet."

"Then we got to find the pictures," Murphy said.

"I want to think about that angle a little," Carmody said.

"We got something good here, Mike. This is what Delaney had on Ackerman. He must know about Dobbs. And that pressure was strong enough to make Ackerman take the big risk of killing your brother. So if we get Dobbs' pictures we get Bill Ackerman. On a rap he can't beat."

"That's it." Carmody glanced at Murphy's tired profile. "You'd have made a good cop, George."

"So would you, Mike," Murphy said. Then he rubbed

his lips with the back of his hand. "Forget that; okay? It's no time for cracks."

"Nobody's mad," Carmody said bitterly.

They said good-by in front of the house and Carmody went inside and tossed his hat on the piano. He was on his way to the kitchen for a beer when the phone began to ring. Picking it up, he said, "Yes?"

"Mike, this is Karen. The police took me downtown this morning to look at more pictures. There was no guard here while I was away." Her voice began to tremble. "Nancy's gone, Mike."

"Who picked you up?" he said sharply.

"A Captain Green. From the records station."

Green was on Ackerman's leash, Carmody knew. Technically, he had the right to bring a witness downtown . . . And someone else could have pulled off the police guard . . . Carmody swore furiously.

"Stay right there," he said. "I'm coming over."

Nancy might have walked out by herself, he thought, as he ran down to his car. But in his heart he knew he was kidding himself. This was Ackerman's work. He wanted her and he had taken her.

12

IT WAS TWENTY minutes later when he reached Karen's apartment. She let him in and sat down on the edge of the sofa, locking her hands together in her lap.

"I've got to know just when this happened," he said. "Right to the minute."

"I'll try to remember."

Carmody saw that she was holding herself under control with an effort. Her small face was pale and strained, and her lower lip was trembling slightly. "If you can hang on you'll be helping her," he said. Sitting beside her, he took her clenched hands between his and rubbed them gently. "Start from the time the police picked you up here."

"That was ten o'clock. Captain Green got here then and said he wanted me to come downtown. I told him I'd get ready. Nancy was frightened. She didn't want to stay alone, but I said it would be all right." Karen drew a long breath and a little tremor went through her body. "I didn't get back until two-thirty. Captain Green showed me dozens of pictures and took his time about it. When we got back he made me wait downstairs until he radioed the local district and told them to put the police details back at the apartment. That was the first I knew that they'd been taken off. I was scared then. And when I came in I saw that she was gone."

Carmody looked around the room. "Was there any sign of a struggle?"

"No. But she left a diamond ring on the basin in the bathroom." Her hands tightened in his. "Wouldn't she have taken that if she decided to walk out?"

"I don't know. She might have forgotten it." Carmody didn't believe this and he saw that Karen didn't either. "We'll find her," he said, squeezing her hand tightly. Then he went quickly to the phone in the kitchen and dialed Police. It took him a minute to get through to Wilson. "Jim, Mike Carmody," he said. "I want to report a missing person. It could be a kidnap job"

"I've been trying to get you, Mike. You've got to come in. Myerdahl didn't buy my brief on you. He insists—"

"Jim, hold that, will you?" Carmody said. "This is the lead to Ackerman. Let's get it rolling. We can talk about Myerdahl later."

Wilson hesitated. Then he said, "Let's have it," in his crisp official voice.

"The missing person is a girl, Nancy Drake. She's blonde with blue eyes and a good figure. About five-three, a hundred and ten, I'd say."

"Nancy Drake? Isn't that Dan Beaumonte's mistress?"

"That's right. She left, or was kidnapped from, the Empire Hotel this morning, sometime between ten o'clock and two-thirty."

"The Empire? That's Karen Stephanson's hotel, right?"

"Yes. I stuck Nancy in her apartment. I thought she'd be safe here with guards at both doors."

"Damn it, what are you trying to do?" Wilson demanded angrily. "Did it occur to you that Beaumonte's girl might have blown the head off our only witness? You said you'd work straight with me, Mike. But you can't drop the prima donna act, even for your brother's murder."

"I guessed wrong," Carmody said. "I didn't figure Ackerman would pull the guard detail off."

"That was a mighty bad guess. Look, now; I'll get an alarm out for this Nancy girl. But you get in here, understand? And bring your badge and gun. Myerdahl wants 'em both."

"Okay," Carmody said bitterly, and replaced the phone with a bang. When he returned to the living room Karen was pacing the floor nervously. "I can't forget that I talked her into helping you," she said.

"This isn't your fault. It's mine."

"She'd just written a letter to her agent," Karen said, putting the palms of her hands against her forehead. "She was sure she'd started back uphill."

"The police of three states will be looking for her," Carmody said. "Remember that." He put his hands gently on her slim square shoulders. "I'll call you as soon as I hear anything," he said.

Carmody walked through the swinging wooden gates of the Homicide Bureau twenty minutes later, and nodded to Dirksen and Abrams who were working at their desks with a suspicious show of industry. Dirksen pointed to Wilson's closed door and said softly, "Very high-priced help at work, Mike. Myerdahl and the D.A."

Carmody smiled faintly at him and rapped on the door. Wilson opened it and said, "Come on in, Mike."

"Anything on the girl yet?"

"No, but the alarm is out."

Carmody walked into the office and took off his hat. Captain Myerdahl, acting superintendent of the department, sat in a straight chair beside Wilson's desk, puffing on a short black pipe. Standing at the windows was Lansing Powell, the city's District Attorney. Myerdahl was a short stocky man with a coarse dark complexion, and small blue eyes that glittered like splinters of ice behind his rimless glasses. He was a tough and shrewd cop, who took his responsibilities with fanatic intensity. As a rookie he had supported his wife and family on two-thirds of his meager salary and spent the remainder on Berlitz lessons to modify his heavy German accent. He had moved up slowly through the ranks, never compromising his standards, and giving every job the full measure of his dogged strength and intelligence. Detectives and patrolmen hated the discipline he enforced but they relished working for him; in Myerdahl's district a cop could do his job twenty-four hours a day without worrying about stepping on sensitive toes.

Myerdahl stood solidly behind his men when they were doing honest work, and he couldn't be intimidated by threats or pressure. Now he looked up at Carmody and took the pipe from his mouth. "I asked the lieutenant for an unfitness report on you this morning," he said bluntly. "But I didn't get it. Instead I got some excuses. Well, I don't take excuses. I've got no use for wealthy cops. They're in the wrong business. So you better find another one."

Carmody's expression remained impassive. "They

should have tied a can to me years ago," he said. "Was that all you had to say?"

"That's all I got to say."

"How about listening to me then?" Carmody said quietly. "I've got a case against Bill Ackerman. I want to give it to you."

"Hah! You think I'd believe you?"

"Forget about me. Listen to the facts. Ackerman's your target, isn't he?"

"I'll get him with men who aren't carrying his money."

"Now just a minute," Powell said, cutting calmly through the tension. "I'm interested in Carmody's information, Superintendent." He came around Wilson's desk, a tall, slender man who wore horn-rimmed glasses and conservative clothes. There was a scholarly, good-humored air about him, the intangible endowment of a good family, excellent schools and a background of noteworthy achievement in the law and politics. But his graceful manners camouflaged a shrewd and vigorous intelligence, as dozens of defense attorneys had learned to their clients' dismay. Perching on the corner of Wilson's desk, he smiled impersonally at Carmody. "In my job I'm forced to use instruments of dubious moral value," he said. "I understand the superintendent's position, but I can't afford the philosophic luxury of observing absolute standards. Call it fighting fire with fire, or whatever you like. I don't justify it or condemn it. It is a condition I accept. However, let me say this much, without any personal rancor, I don't like using crooked cops. To me they're a lost and frightening breed of men, and I would prefer to keep as far away from them as possible." He studied Carmody's hard impassive face, a curious frown gathering about his eyes. "You're what some people call a smart operator, I suppose. I've known others like you, and I think I understand your reasoning processes. When you join the force it occurs to you in time that there is a way to make the job pay off more handsomely than the taxpayers intended. In short, to cheat, to trade on your position of public trust. What doesn't occur to you is that the same course is open to every man in the department. They can cheat, or play it straight. Thank God, most of them play it straight. But you don't give them credit for that. You see their honesty as stupidity, their integrity as a lack of nerve. This is why I find you rather frightening." Powell shrugged and crossed his long legs. But he was still frowning thoughtfully at Carmody. "You rationalize your dishonesty with more of the same deadly cynicism," he said slowly. "You say, 'If I don't take the graft then someone else will.' This isn't logic, of course, it's merely an expression of your lack of faith. If you were logical you would test the proposition by being honest. Instead, you simply assume that everyone else is dishonest. You prejudge the world by yourself and steal with the comforting defense that you're only beating the other crooks to it. The thing you—"

"That's an excellent speech, sir," Carmody said abruptly. "I'd like to hear the rest of it sometime. I mean that. But *I* want to talk now."

Powell nodded. "Okay, Carmody. What have you to tell us?"

"A story about a man named Dobbs. A man Ackerman is afraid of." He gave it to them in rapid detail, his trained mind presenting each fact in its damaging order. When he finished the attitude of the men facing him had changed; Wilson was grinning with excitement, Myerdahl had hunched forward to the edge of his chair and Powell was walking back and forth before the desk with a grim little look on his face. And the atmosphere of the room had changed, too; it was charged now with excitement and tension.

"Well," Carmody said, "is it a case?"

"It may very well be," Powell said. "It's a logical inference that Dobbs took photographs of Ackerman participating in a robbery and murder. The robbery isn't important, but the murder can still send him to the chair. And I'm quite sure that Dobbs has taken every precaution to make his case against Ackerman airtight. The pictures are probably in a vault, and his attorney probably has a letter instructing him to present them to the police in the event anything sudden and fatal happens to Dobbs. Ackerman must be efficiently trapped, or he wouldn't have paid off all these years. He would simply have shot him. So our job is to find the pictures."

"We can get them," Myerdahl said, thumping the desk with his fist. "A court order can open vaults. And we'll smoke out his lawyer. Or if the letter is with his family, we'll drag them back and make them talk."

"It will finish Ackerman," Powell said, turning to Carmody. "But it doesn't touch Beaumonte or the organization."

"I can wrap them up for you," Carmody said.

"How's that?"

"I've got a witness they won't like," Carmody said. "A man who knows every name, every date and every pay-off connected with the city's rackets. He's been on Beaumonte's payroll for six years and he's willing to talk. Can you use him?"

"I most certainly can," Powell said. "Who is he?"

"Me," Carmody said quietly.

A silence grew and stretched in the smoky room. Wilson let out his breath slowly and Myerdahl rubbed his jaw and studied Carmody suspiciously. "Well," Powell said at last. "You'll be an almighty big help. But since there's a good chance you'll go to jail, why are you doing this?"

"I'm tired of that question," Carmody said, shrugging his wide shoulders. "And what difference does it make? If we get a case, what else matters?"

"Several things," Powell said, smiling slightly. "The most important thing, however, is to make men like you recognize the difference between right and wrong, to make you realize that you're responsible for understanding the distinction. We can get Ackerman and Beaumonte a good deal easier than the border-line cases who support them by a cynical indifference to their moral obligations. That's why I'm interested in your motive. Is it just a grudge? Or is something a little different, a little better perhaps?"

Carmody was about to speak when the phone rang. Wilson picked it up and said, "Yes, go ahead." He listened a moment, a slow frown spreading over his face, and then he nodded and said shortly, "Let me know the minute anything else comes in." Replacing the phone he looked at Carmody. "That might be Nancy Drake, Mike. Radio has picked up a report from a New Jersey traffic car. They've got an accident a mile south of Exit 21 on the Turnpike. The victim fits the description of Nancy Drake. But the identification isn't positive."

"It's positive," Carmody said slowly. "They took her out and killed her. Because she gave me the lead that may hang them." There was no anger in him, only a cold and terrible determination. He looked from Powell to Myerdahl, breathing slowly and deeply. "You two did all the talking so far," he said. "Now listen: while you were talking they killed her like they'd swat a fly. Dobbs will be next, then me, then any other fool who gets in their way. They know they can get away with it because while their guns are banging you sit talking and drowning out the noise. There's no case against them here, there's nothing but talk. And I'm sick of it. You treated me like a leper because I wanted to help and I'm sick of that, too. Now I'm going to settle this without any more conversation."

Carmody backed toward the door and Wilson said, "Don't go off half-cocked, Mike."

"More talk," Carmody said, smiling unpleasantly. "Keep it up! Mr. Powell, tell them about right and wrong and the evil in the city's scout packs. Myerdahl, come up with some stories of your early days as a cop. Talk your heads off, but for God's sake don't do anything."

"I'd suggest you relax if I thought it would do any good," Powell said pleasantly.

"You're suspended!" Myerdahl shouted, leaping to his feet.

"You're suspended, too," Carmody said. "In a big tub of virtuous incompetence. Maybe that's why I went crooked. Because I got tired of you good little people who can't get anything done."

He walked out and pulled the door shut behind him with an explosive bang.

State troopers had channeled all northbound traffic into one lane to by-pass the scene of the accident. The darkness was split by the red lights of squad cars parked on the grass off the highway. Carmody pulled up behind them and walked down to the gully where a fire-blackened convertible lay upside down, its wheels pointing grotesquely and helplessly at the sky. Men were working around it, measuring skid tracks, beginning the tests on brakes, wheel alignment, ignition system. A uniformed patrolman stood beside a small, blanket-covered figure on the ground. Carmody walked over to him and said, "Has the doctor gone?"

"Yes. He couldn't do anything. What's your business?" he added.

"Metropolitan police," Carmody said opening his wallet. "I want to check an identification."

"Sure, Sarge. Go ahead."

Carmody knelt down and drew the blanket gently away from the small figure on the ground. He stared at her a moment, his face grim and hard in the flaring shadows thrown by the police lights. The fire, rather miraculously, hadn't touched her face or hair. She must have crawled halfway out the window before the smoke and flame got her, he thought. For half a moment he stared at the frozen, inanimate pain on her face, at the leaves and twigs caught in her tangled blonde hair. He kept his eyes away from the rest of her body. You didn't get back to show business, he thought. You just got murdered. He put the blanket over her face and got to his feet.

"Do you know what happened?" he asked the uniformed cop.

"I heard the talk," the cop said respectfully; the look in Carmody's face made him anxious to help. "She was alone in the car when the first motorist got to her and pulled her out. But nobody saw the crash. She lost control about fifty yards from the bridge, judging from the skid tracks. Then she barreled down here and tipped over."

It was phony all the way, Carmody knew. Nancy had never been behind the wheel of a car in her life.

"She didn't have much of a chance," the cop said, and shook his head.

"Not a ghost."

Carmody walked up the grade to his car. The single line of traffic passed him on his left, moving slowly despite the shouted orders from the troopers. Everyone wants a glimpse of tragedy, he thought, while faces peered out of the slowly moving cars, eager for the sounds and smells of disaster. Carmody looked down the hill at the blanket-draped figure on the ground, and then he slipped his car into gear and headed back to the city.

Half an hour later he rapped on the door of Beaumonte's apartment. Footsteps sounded and Beaumonte, in his shirt-sleeves, opened the door the big padded roll of his body swelling tightly against the waistband of his trousers. Without a jacket he didn't look formidable; he was just another fat man in a silk shirt and loud suspenders.

"I'm in kind of a hurry, Mike," he said, not moving aside. "What's on your mind?"

The long room behind was empty and Carmody saw three pigskin bags in the middle of the floor. "You're taking a trip?" he said.

"That's right." Beaumonte's smile was a grudging concession which didn't relieve the annoyance in his face. "I'm catching a plane in half an hour."

"You asked me to find Nancy," Carmody said. He walked into the room, forcing Beaumonte to step aside, and tossed his hat in a chair.

"Well, where is she?" Beaumonte asked him anxiously.

Carmody faced him with his hands on his hips. "She's under a blanket, Dan. They pulled her out of a wreck on the Turnpike about an hour ago. She's dead."

"Dead?" Beaumonte stared at him incredulously. "No, you're kidding," he whispered. His face had turned white and his lips were beginning to tremble. "She can't be dead," he said, shaking his head quickly.

"I saw her. She burned to death."

Beaumonte put both hands over his face and lurched blindly toward the sofa. He sat down, his body sprawling slackly on the cushions, and began to cry in a soft, anguished voice.

Carmody lit a cigarette and flipped the m the ashtray. He watched Beaumonte's effo self under control with no expression at all on his face.

"I loved that girl," Beaumonte said, in a choking voice. His eyes were closed but tears welled under the lids and coursed slowly down his white cheeks. "I loved her and she never looked at another guy. She was all mine. Where did it happen? Who was with her?"

"She was alone," Carmody said.

It took several seconds for this to register. When it did, Beaumonte opened his eyes and struggled up to a sitting position. "She never drove, she couldn't," he said hoarsely. "What are you saying, Mike?"

"She was murdered," Carmody said.

Beaumonte shook his head so quickly that tears were shaken from his fat cheeks. "Ackerman said he wouldn't hurt her," he cried in a rising voice. "He said he wouldn't touch her."

"And you believed him. Like I believed you when you said you'd give Eddie forty-eight hours."

"Why did he kill her?" Beaumonte said, mumbling the words through his trembling lips. "He didn't have to do that. I could have kept her quiet."

"She was killed because she told me about Dobbs," Carmody said coldly. "That's going to hang Ackerman. And it may hang you, too, Dan."

Beaumonte began to weep. "Mike, please. I been through enough."

"You've put hundreds of people on the same rack," Carmody said bitterly. "I could laugh at you if you were lying in hell with your back broken. Now get this: you and Ackerman are going down the drain and I helped pull the plug. I'm going with you, but that seems a fair price. You can sweat out the next six months in jail, or you can die right now. The choice is yours."

"What do you mean?"

Carmody took out his revolver and shoved the barrel deep into Beaumonte's wide stomach. "I want the name of the guy who killed my brother," he said gently. "And his address."

"Ackerman made the plans," Beaumonte said, his voice going up in a squeal. "He got a guy named Joie Langley from Chicago."

"Is he still in town?"

Beaumonte wet his lips as he stared into Carmody's cold gray eyes. "Don't shoot, Mike," he whispered. "I'm talking. Langley's staying in a rooming house on Broome Street. The address is 4842. Ackerman didn't want him to leave while there was a witness who could finger him. If he couldn't get rid of the witness, then he planned to get rid of Langley. Langley's got no money at all, and he can't move. He's a bad kid, Mike."

"I'll make an angel out of him," Carmody said, putting away his gun. "Now don't move until I'm gone."

When the door closed Beaumonte struggled to his feet, breathing heavily, his eyes glistening with tears. Sweat was streaming down his body, plastering his silk shirt to the slabs of flesh that armored his ribs. He walked around the room, wandering in a circle, occasionally moaning like a man goaded by an intense, recurring pain. Finally, he went to the telephone, lifted the receiver and dialed a number. Staring at the wall, he wet his lips and attempted desperately to get himself under control.

A voice said, "Yes?"

"Ackerman? This is Dan."

"I thought you'd gone. I told you the ceiling was ready to fall in," Ackerman told him shortly.

"Carmody's picking up Joie Langley, Bill. He's spread the story about Dobbs. Now he's after his brother's killer. I thought you'd like to know."

"Is he alone?"

"Yes." Beaumonte put the phone down abruptly and walked to the bar. While he was making himself a strong drink the phone began to ring. Beaumonte stared at it and sipped his drink. He wasn't crying any more; his pale face was set in a haggard expression of hate. "Go after him, Bill," he whispered to the ringing phone. "He'll pay you off for me, he'll send you to hell."

13

BROOME STREET stretched from the river to the heart of the city and terminated in a dead end a half-block below the Municipal Building. Its upper section was smart and prosperous, with excellent shops and department stores facing each other across a broad asphalt surface. But the street changed character as it wound through warehouses and slums to the river. Overhead lights gave way to street lamps set far apart, and the gutters were clotted with newspapers, garbage and refuse. The tall, red brick buildings had been converted into rooming houses for dock laborers, and the neon signs of cheap bars glittered at every corner.

Carmody parked in the 4800 block and when he switched off the motor a dark thick silence settled around him. The warehouses and garages were locked up at this hour, and the dawn-rising longshoremen were in bed for the night. Moving quietly, he walked down the empty sidewalk to number 4842, a narrow, four-storied brick building, identical with a dozen others in the block. He ascended the short stoop of stone stairs, hollowed by decades of use, and tried the door. It was locked, as he'd expected it would be. He rang the night bell.

A few minutes later a stockily built Irishman wearing

only a pair of trousers peered out at him with sleepy, belligerent eyes.

"Now what's your pleasure?" he said.

Carmody held out his badge and let the slanting light from the hallway fall on it. "Talk as natural as you can," he said quietly. "Answer my questions. Have you got a spare room?"

The man cleared his throat and stared at the badge. "We're all full up," he said.

"Think I'd have better luck somewhere else in the block?"

"Couldn't say for sure. You can try across the street, at 4839. They might have an extra."

"A big blond man with a wide face," Carmody said quietly. "If he's here nod your head."

The man's eyes became round and solemn. He nodded slowly and jerked his thumb in a furtive gesture to his right. "Just beside me," he said, breathing out the words. "Front room."

"Thanks, anyway," Carmody said, and moved silently past him into the small airless hallway. He closed the front door and pointed to the stairs. The man needed no urging; he took the steps two at a time, his bare feet noiseless on the faded carpet.

Carmody waited until he had turned out of sight at the second-floor landing. Then he rapped sharply on the door of the front room. His breathing was even and slow, and his hands hung straight down at his sides.

Bedsprings creaked beyond the door and footsteps moved across the floor.

"Who's that?" a voice said quietly.

"Message from Bill Ackerman," Carmody said.

The door opened an inch and stopped. Carmody saw one eye shining softly from the light in the hallway, and below that the cold blue glint of a gun barrel.

"Walk straight in when I open the door," the voice said. "Stop in the middle of the room and don't turn around. Get that straight."

"Okay, I've got it."

"Start walking."

The door swung open. Carmody entered the dark room with the hall light shining on his back. He was a perfect target if the killer wanted to shoot. But he wasn't worried about that. Not yet.

A switch clicked and a bare bulb above his head flooded the room with white harsh light. He heard the door swing shut, a lock click and then a gun barrel pressed hard against his spine. The man's free hand went over him with expert speed, found his revolver and flipped it free of the holster.

"Take off your hat now," he said. "Real slow. Raise it with both hands."

He knows his racket, Carmody thought, lifting his hat. Occasionally even a cop might forget that a small gun could be carried on the top of a man's head under a fedora.

"Lemme look at you now," the man said.

Turning slowly, Carmody faced the man who had killed his brother. Look down here, Eddie, he prayed. This is for you.

"You're Joie Langley, right?" he said quietly.

"Don't make conversation. What's with Ackerman?"

Langley's youth surprised Carmody. He was twenty-four, or twenty-five at most, a big muscular kid with tousled blond hair and sullen eyes set close together in a wide brutal face. The gun he held looked like a finger of his huge hand. He was wearing loafers, slacks and an unbuttoned yellow sports shirt that exposed his solid hairy chest. About Eddie's age, Carmody thought, but a different breed. He was a hard and savage killer; Eddie wouldn't have had a chance with him, even from the front.

"Ackerman wants you to clear out," Carmody said. "I'm a cop, and I work for him. I'll set it up for you."

"A cop?" Langley said softly, and took a step back from Carmody. He went down in a springy crouch, his sullen eyes narrowing with suspicion. "I don't like this, buddy. The whole deal stinks. I'm the hottest guy in the country but he won't pay off, won't let me clear out. Where's your badge, buddy?"

"I'll take my wallet from my hip pocket," Carmody said quietly. "I'll do it nice and slow. You're getting all excited, sonny. What's the matter? This your first job?"

Langley swore at him impersonally. Then he said, "I'm making sure it ain't my last, that's all. Take out your frontpiece."

Carmody opened his wallet and flashed the badge. "Look at the name on the identification card," he said. "That's important, too."

Langley stared at him, the gun steady in his big fist. "I like this less all the time, buddy," he said.

"You'd be spending your dough in Las Vegas right

now if you hadn't fumbled the job," Carmody said. "Look at the name in that wallet. Then we'll get moving."

Langley took the wallet in his free hand and held it at eye-level. He was still watching Carmody. "You sound like you think you're tough," he said casually.

"Look at the name."

Langley grinned and glanced at the identification card, keeping the gun fixed steadily on Carmody's stomach.

"Michael T. Carmody," he said, reading the name slowly. A puzzled line deepened above his eyes. "That's the name of the guy I—"

Carmody had raised his hand casually—as if he were going to scratch his chin—and now he struck down at Langley's wrist, gambling on the hoodlum's momentary confusion and the speed and power of his own body.

He almost lost his bet.

Langley jerked back from the blow, his lips flattening in a snarl, and the rock-hard edge of Carmody's hand missed his wrist—but it struck the top of his thumb and knocked his finger away from the trigger. For a split second the gun dangled impotently in his hand, and Carmody made another desperate bet on himself and whipped a left hook into Langley's face. It would have been safer to try for the gun; if the hook missed he'd be dead before he could throw another punch. But it didn't miss; Langley's head snapped back as Carmody's fist exploded under his jaw and the gun spun from his hand to the floor. Carmody kicked it under the bed and began to laugh. Then he hit Langley in the stomach with a right that raised him two inches off the floor. When

Langley bent over, gasping for breath, Carmody brought his knee up into his face and knocked him halfway across the room.

"It was your last job, sonny," he said, grabbing the slack of the sports shirt and pulling him to his feet. "You shot a good kid, my brother. But you shoot nobody else."

Langley stared at him, breathing raggedly, hate shining from his bleeding ruined face. "I'd cut off my hands and feet for one chance at you, copper," he cried softly. "I'd fix you good."

"You had your chance, sonny," Carmody said. "A thousand more wouldn't help." Turning Langley around, he twisted his wrist up between his shoulder blades and locked it there in the vise of his own big hand. "Eddie could have taken you front to front," he said. "You're not big-time, you're all mouth. We're going downtown now and I'll turn you over to my brother's friends. If you want your troubles to start sooner just get balky. I'll break this arm of yours off and make you carry it."

"I don't scare, copper," Langley said angrily.

Carmody hesitated in the bleak room and stared with bitter eyes into his own past. "No, we don't scare, sonny," he said. "God Himself can't scare us. So we wind up like this. Little men begging for a break."

"Who's little?"

"You're little enough to fit in the chair," Carmody said. "That's what counts. How old are you?"

"Twenty-six my next birthday."

"A ripe old age," Carmody said, and sighed. "Let's go."

He retrieved his revolver, opened the door and shoved Langley out into the dimly lighted hallway. The house was still and quiet. It was just about all over, Carmody knew, and he was restless and impatient for the final end of it. The power and drive that had always been a pressure within him seemed to be gone; even his anger had watered down to a heavy pervading bitterness. He was reaching for the knob when the doorbell broke clamorously through the silence.

Carmody froze, tightening his grip on Langley's wrist.

"Easy now," he whispered.

"Maybe you got trouble, copper."

"You'll get it first."

Carmody was in an awkward position. With one hand he couldn't open the door and still keep an effective grip on the gun. And Langley might break if he put away the gun to open the door.

"Maybe we got action," Langley said, laughing soundlessly.

"You won't see it," Carmody said; raising his gun he slugged him at the base of the skull, not hard enough to injure him but hard enough to silence him for a few moments. Langley sagged against him and Carmody caught his arms and lowered him to the floor.

Then he turned the knob, releasing the catch, and stepped quickly back to the shadow of the stairs. The door swung open and Myers, the little detective from his shift, walked into the hallway.

"Good Lord," he said closing the door quickly, and glancing from Carmody down to Langley's sprawled body.

"How did you find me?" Carmody said.

Myers was breathing rapidly, his small cautious face tense with excitement. "That can wait, Mike. Ackerman's sitting across the street in his car. With Hymie Schmidt. Did you know that?"

Carmody felt a quiver of excitement go down his spine. It wasn't over yet; not by a long sight. Ackerman was the man he had come closer to fearing than anyone else he had known in his life. And now Ackerman was waiting for him.

"There's an alarm out for him," Myers said. "He's wanted for questioning. And he's on the run."

"How did you know I was here?"

"I spotted your car down the block. That old mobster at my wife's sanitarium gave me the tip on this guy." He glanced down at Langley. "Someone in Chicago told him a guy named Joie Langley had come east to do a job on a cop. A pet stoolie of mine tipped me off he was staying here. I came out just to look around and then I saw your car. That scared me. So I decided to come in. That's when I saw Ackerman and Schmidt pull up and stop across the street."

"They've seen my car, too, then," Carmody said. "We don't have much time. They'll either clear out or come in here shooting."

"I got it all thought out," Myers said, gripping his arm. "They don't know me from Adam. To them I'm just a little guy who lives here or is hunting for a room. Well, look: I'll walk out again and go down to the sidewalk. I take out cigarettes, pretend I need a match and cross the street to their car. When I get there I put my gun in their face. And that's the end of it. You can cover me from here. Okay?"

Carmody hesitated. It was a good bold move but Myers wasn't the man for it. "No," he said.

"It will work."

"What the devil are you trying to prove?"

Myers shook his head slowly. "They killed a cop, remember? I'm going to prove they can't get away with it. That's what's important to me. Don't you ever know what makes people tick, Mike?"

"No, I'm too dumb," Carmody said wearily. Then he put his hand awkwardly on Myers' shoulder. "Forgive me, will you? You're a better cop than I could be in a thousand years. Go out and arrest those bastards."

"You watch me." Myers opened the door and went down the stone steps to the sidewalk. From the crack of the partially open door Carmody saw Ackerman's long black car parked across the street, and the faces of the two men in the front seat, pale triangular blurs in the darkness. He watched Myers fumble through his pockets, bring out cigarettes and stick one in his mouth. Weaving slightly, Myers dug around again in his pockets for matches. Carmody felt perspiration starting on his forehead; the little detective was overdoing it, playing it like a drunk on a stage. But it was too late to drag him back. Myers had started across the street to Ackerman's car, weaving on rubbery legs.

"You guys got a match?" Carmody heard him call.

"I think so." It was Ackerman's voice, carrying clearly across the silent street.

"Good guy," Myers said, laughing cheerfully.

That was when Ackerman shot him, as he approached the car, doing his imitation of a drunk's lurching walk. The report blasted the silence and sent shattering echoes racing along the dark blocks.

Carmody charged down to the sidewalk as he saw Myers fall, and heard his shrill incredulous cry of pain. His gun banged twice and the glass in Ackerman's windshield shattered with a noisy crash. He saw Ackerman clearly then but before he could fire again something struck his shoulder and spun his body around in a full circle. There was no pain at first, only the incredible, sledge-hammer impact of the bullet. He was on his knees, feeling for his gun when the pain hit, driving into him like a white-hot needle. The breath left his body in a squeezing rush and he put a hand quickly on the pavement to keep himself from falling on his face. When he raised his head, Ackerman was standing above him, looking as tall as the buildings. "You rotten filthy dog," he said, staring at Carmody with furious eyes. "You fixed me good. But you're where you belong now, on your knees and ready to die."

Carmody fought against a dizzying pain and nausea. "You're through," he grinned, and the effort stretched the skin whitely across his cheekbones. "It wasn't a bad night's work."

"I'll be alive when you're dead," Ackerman said, his voice trembling with passion.

Windows had gone up along the block and from a distance came the faint baying of a police siren.

"Boss, let's go," Hymie Schmidt shouted from inside the car.

"Just one more second," Ackerman said, putting the cold muzzle of his gun against Carmody's forehead. "Don't worry about me," he said, leaning forward and speaking slowly and clearly. "I've got judges and lawyers in every pocket. And shooting a crooked cop is an easy rap to beat."

"Damn you!" Hymie Schmidt yelled, and let out the clutch with a snap. The car shot forward with a deep roar of power. Ackerman spun around, his face twisting with alarm. "Stop!" he shouted, and ran a few yards down the street, waving both arms in the air. Finally, he halted, cursing furiously at the fading tail-light.

When he turned around, Carmody was kneeling as he had left him, but Myers was sitting up in the street with a gun in his lap, his little face frozen and white with pain.

"You won't kill any more cops," he said weakly, and shot Ackerman through the head.

14

A POLICE CAR took Carmody to St. David's Hospital where a doctor cut away his shirt, removed the bullet and dressed the wound in his shoulder. Afterward, Carmody sat on a bench in the starkly clean accident ward and smoked a cigarette. He felt empty and drained but in a little while strength began flowing sluggishly back into his body.

"Hell, man, you're indestructible," an intern said, as Carmody got slowly to his feet.

"Don't bet on that," Carmody said. The uniformed cop who was waiting to drive him to Headquarters put a coat gently over his bare shoulders. "Ready, Sarge?" he asked.

"We'll wait until we hear about Myers," Carmody said.

A nurse came down from the operating room a few minutes later. "How's he making it?" he asked her.

The nurse was a pretty girl with soft warm eyes and something about Carmody made her feel like taking him in her arms. For all his size and toughness he seemed so bewildered and lost.

"He has a chance," she said.

"How good?"

"Pretty good, I think."

"Thank you."

"You're welcome," the nurse said, and touched his arm timidly.

Carmody smiled at her, then glanced at the cop. "Let's roll," he said.

The record room at Homicide was jammed with police and reporters, and the noise of their excited, splintered conversations rumbled through the smoky air. There was an uproar when Carmody came in. Reporters on dead line tried to get to him for any kind of statement, but Abrams begged them to shut up and clear the hell out of the way. "You'll get your stories," he shouted, circling Carmody like an indignant hen. "But give us a break first, for the Lord's sake."

Over the heads of the crowd Carmody saw Karen and George Murphy standing against the wall. She stood on tiptoes, watching him anxiously, and Murphy was patting her shoulder with a big clumsy hand. Abrams took Carmody's good arm and said, "They want you in Wilson's office, Mike."

"Just a second." Carmody pushed through the ring of reporters and cops and walked over to Karen. "Can you stick around?" he asked her. "I'm going to be busy for a while."

"Yes, I'll wait. Are you all right?"

"What? Oh, sure." He glanced down at the splint and sling on his arm. "It's not bad." He felt suddenly as if he were walking through a dream. "Did you identify Langley?"

She nodded and wet her lips. He saw that she was very pale. "The police took me to see him a few minutes ago."

"You'll stick around?" he said, frowning slightly.

"Yes, Mike."

Murphy smiled at him and patted his shoulder gently. "It's a great story. 'Cop Nabs Brother's Slayer.' The copy desks can ring some beautiful changes on that one."

"Wouldn't it be nice if that's the way it was," Carmody said.

"Yes, that would be pretty," Murphy said with a little sigh. "Well, I'll see you later, Mike."

"You'll get the whole story, George. That was the deal."

"Sure, I'm not worried. Take it easy, pal."

"I'll see you as soon as I can," Carmody said to Karen. "You'll be here?" Even in his confusion he realized he was pressing the point with absurd insistence.

"Yes, Mike."

Wilson's office, in comparison to the record room, seemed like a haven of peace. Myerdahl and Powell were talking together at the window, and Wilson was seated at his desk. When Carmody came in Wilson jumped to his feet, grinning with pleasure and excitement, and led him to a chair. "It was a fine night's work, Mike," he said. "The best we've had since I've been in the department. How're you feeling?"

"Pretty good, I guess."

Powell sauntered over and patted Carmody's shoulder. "I'll say amen to Jimmy's comment," he said. "It was a great night's work. We've got your brother's killer and Ackerman is dead. The organization is in for a terrific thump."

"How about Beaumonte?"

"He caught a plane for Miami a few hours ago. But Langley has already confessed that Beaumonte hired him to do the job on your brother. So we'll bring Mr. Beaumonte back on a murder charge. We still haven't found the pictures Dobbs was using to blackmail Ackerman, but they've already served their purpose. They made him stampede."

Carmody fumbled for a cigarette and discovered he had none. Powell brought out his case quickly. "Have one of these?"

"Thanks." Carmody blew a stream of smoke at the floor and rubbed his forehead. He could feel fatigue settling on him with a ponderous pressure. "I wonder how Ackerman knew I was going to get Langley?"

Wilson said, "Hymie Schmidt answered that for us. Beaumonte tipped off Ackerman you were going out there."

Carmody sighed wearily. "He used me as his executioner. I was still on the payroll."

The mood in the room changed slightly. Powell looked at his watch and said, "I've got to get up to my office. We'll be working all night, as it is."

Myerdahl took the short black pipe from his mouth and said bluntly, "I don't take back my words this afternoon, Carmody. But I say this now. You were all cop tonight."

Carmody smiled faintly. "Thanks, Superintendent."

When they had gone Wilson sat on the edge of his desk and drew a long breath. He studied Carmody for a few seconds in silence. Then he said lightly, "The peace and quiet is kind of a relief, isn't it?"

"Peace?" Carmody said, smiling crookedly. "Where is it, Jim?" He sat slumped in the chair, head bowed, staring at the cracks in the floor. The overhead light gleamed on his thick blond hair, on the hard flat planes of his face, on the white sling stretching diagonally across his bare chest. Sighing, he shook his head slowly. "I was wrong, Jim," he said. Karen had told him to say that, he remembered. And had warned him that the words might choke. But nothing like that happened. It was a relief to say the words. It was like putting down an intolerable burden. "Yes, I was wrong," he murmured. What came next? You asked for forgiveness, that was it. He'd done that, he recalled, he'd asked Myers to forgive him. But it didn't seem enough. He hadn't changed; no bells of hope pealed in his soul, no promise of salvation blazed before his eyes. Maybe what Father Ahearn had suggested fitted in here. Come back little by little. The way he'd gone away.

"What will happen to me, Jim?" he said quietly. He was curious about that in an impersonal manner; it didn't really matter because the big thing had already happened. He knew he was ruined. The mainspring that was the core of his strength had been smashed. Goodness had destroyed him. And that was almost comical. Mike Carmody had been hunted down, surrounded and destroyed. Cops like Myers and Wilson, women like Nancy and Karen, even big fat George Murphy had been in on the kill. He had thought they were fools, pushovers, weaklings—looking at them but seeing himself—and they ˙d calmly smashed him to bits with their decency and goodness. Everything he believed had been proven invalid. So what was left of Mike Carmody?

Wilson came over beside him and put a hand on his shoulder. "Damn it, we all make mistakes," he said, hunting awkwardly for words. "Don't let this thing beat you all the way down, Mike. What will happen to you is anybody's guess. The papers will play you up as the fearless cop who avenged his brother's murder. When the rest of it comes out, that you were on Ackerman's team, well they may switch around and make you out the biggest bum in the city. Powell is on your side though, and so is Myerdahl, if he'll ever admit it." Wilson frowned and then rubbed a hand over his face. "The best thing you can hope for is that they'll let you resign without pressing charges."

So I'm through as a cop, Carmody thought, still staring at the floor. That had been important once, but now it didn't matter. Nothing mattered really. He felt as if his body and soul were vacuums, drained and empty, without even a promise of hope to sustain them.

"What's the worst I can expect?" he asked.

Wilson shrugged. Reluctantly he said, "Three, four years, maybe."

"Am I under arrest?"

"No, but you'll have to stick around. Powell wants me to take a statement from you tonight on your connection with Beaumonte and Ackerman."

"That fast?"

"We've got to do it fast. Before the organization can grow another head."

"Okay. Can I go outside and say good-by to a friend?"

"Sure, of course."

The record room had returned to its normal state of quiet efficiency; the reporters had gone up with Powell to work on the story of Ackerman's death and the patrolmen had been detailed back to their squads and wagons. Abrams was at his desk, studying a file, and the clerk was typing out a report, occasionally pausing to stare through the dirty windows at the dark city. The bright overhead light was merciless on the battered furniture, the cigarette-littered floor, the curling flyers tacked on the bulletin board. It was a room that had been part of Carmody's life for years, but after tonight that would be all over.

Karen sat alone on the wooden bench at the wall, striking an incongruously elegant note against the drab and dusty office. She was wearing a black suit, high-heeled pumps, and her hair was brushed back from her small serious face. Good people, he thought. That had occurred to him before, but grudgingly and suspiciously. Now it was a simple unqualified tribute.

She rose lightly to her feet as he crossed the room.

"Let's sit down," he said. He felt clumsy and constrained with her, hopelessly at a loss for words. "I've just got a few minutes," he said at last. "There's a lot of routine to get out of the way, you know."

"Yes, of course. Don't worry about me, Mike. I'll get a cab."

"Where will you go?"

"Well, I haven't thought about it. Some hotel, probably."

The room was silent except for the occasional rattle of the clerk's typewriter.

"You told me to say I was wrong," he said, dragging the words out with an effort. "I did that. I wanted you to know."

She looked at him gravely. "Did it hurt?"

"It wasn't too bad." He frowned at the floor, feeling weary and helpless. It wouldn't work. There was no way to get to her, no way to bridge the barrier of bitterness he had built between them.

But miraculously, she came to him. "Don't try to do too much all at once," she said, putting a hand on his wrist. "Take it in easy stages. That works, you'll find."

"Look, I was wrong about you," he said. "That was as wrong as I ever got. Can you believe that? Can you forgive me?"

"That won't be hard, Mike. But let's do it the way I suggested. In easy stages. Okay?"

"All right, whatever you say," he said. Then he sighed and looked at the big clock above the police speaker. "The lieutenant's waiting for me."

They walked around the counter together and stopped at the swinging doors that opened on the corridor. "Eddie's funeral is tomorrow morning," he said. "Would you want to go with me?"

"I'd like that, Mike."

"Look, I may be going to jail," he said abruptly. "They can let me resign, or send me up. Either way, can I find you afterwards?"

"You'll be able to find me," she said slowly.

Carmody smiled into her small brave face, and put

a hand on her shoulder. For just that instant there was a suggestion of the old hard confidence in his eyes. "I'll see you, Karen," he said.

"Good-by, Mike," she said in a soft voice, and pushed through the swinging doors and walked quickly down the corridor.

Carmody watched her until she turned out of sight. Standing alone, he stared into the dim empty corridor, still seeing in his mind the graceful swing of her legs and the high proud look of her head and shoulders. After a few moments he shook his head and rubbed his forehead and eyes with the back of his good hand. Then he turned and walked slowly into the record room. The door to the lieutenant's office stood open, and Carmody saw that Wilson was waiting for him, an empty chair pulled up beside his desk.

Carmody wet his lips, suddenly swept by an emotion that he couldn't define. Part of it was fear, but there was something else, too. For a moment he stood indecisively, staring at the empty chair that waited for him at Wilson's elbow. Finally, it came to him; this was what he felt as a child when he waited in the line at the confessional. Fear, yes, but something else. And the other thing was the sweeping relief that came from the anticipation of forgiveness.

Smiling slowly, Carmody walked into the lieutenant's office. "Let's go," he said, and eased himself gratefully into the empty chair.